# MISADVENTURES

## WITH A

# MANNY

BY
TONI ALEO

# MISADVENTURES WITH A MANNY

BY
TONI ALEO

WATERHOUSE PRESS

Copyright © 2018 Waterhouse Press, LLC
Cover Design by Waterhouse Press.
Cover images: Shutterstock

PRINTED IN THE UNITED STATES OF AMERICA

ISBN: 978-1-64263-004-6

*To my dad, Noel.*
*Thank you for always believing in me and being*
*so proud of me. I wouldn't be who I am without you.*
*Love you.*

# CHAPTER ONE

## VERA

I am completely heartbroken.

Everything hurts.

But not due to the loss I am experiencing.

That sickening feeling in my gut is for my boys.

Holding Louis's and Elliot's hands, I watch my soon-to-be ex-husband, Simon, carry boxes to his truck. His girlfriend—Kaia, our former nanny—stands by the back of a cab with a pained look on her face. What the hell she has to be pained about is beyond me. She stole my children's father from them and my husband from me. Yeah, things were rough between Simon and me. I worked a lot, as did he, but I'd loved him since I was sixteen. He is all I know, and now, he is leaving us.

His family.

Placing the boxes in the truck bed, Simon whispers something in her ear, and she gives him a weak smile. I want to scream. I want to throw something at them. How dare he display his love right there in front of our children. I wouldn't do that to my kids.

But I don't say or do anything. I have to stay strong for them. Especially for our oldest, Charlie. He hasn't been handling this well. Not that I expect him to.

Just then, Charlie barrels out of the house. He throws a box onto the lawn, his voice breaking as he screams, "Here you go. Take the rest of your crap!"

"Charlie, that's unnecessary," Simon calls, walking toward our fourteen-year-old son. "You don't need to be hostile. Is your mother hostile?"

Charlie doesn't even look at me. His fists are shaking, his face red. He loves his father. Sometimes, I am convinced he loves his dad more than he loves me. They used to do everything together. Simon isn't a bad father. But not only did he betray me with the affair, he betrayed the trust of our boys. Charlie swings his leg back and kicks Simon's box hard. I press my lips together and stifle the impulse to intervene. This is between them.

Quite honestly, I wish *I* could kick something. My heart sinks as my son makes a scene.

"I hate you. You know that? How can you do this to us? We are supposed to be a family!"

"And we are." Simon reaches for him, but Charlie smacks his father's hands away. "Just because I don't love your mother anymore doesn't mean I don't love you."

Hearing that really stings.

"Well, I don't love you! You're leaving us. For her? She's as dumb as a box of rocks. You've said that yourself."

"Charlie, things change—"

"No! You couldn't keep your dick in your pants, and you ruined everything. You're running out on us, and we don't want you back." He kicks Simon's box again, splitting open the side so the contents spill out. "You're nothing but a piece of shit!" Charlie roars and runs back into the house, slamming the door. Louis and Elliot jump a bit, so I squeeze their hands tightly, fighting back tears. I normally would never let my son talk like that to his father, but I know whatever I'd say would fall on deaf ears. Charlie is too upset, too heartbroken. His pain is killing me, combining with my own pain to form a dangerous mix. How could I let this happen? What did I do wrong? Did I work too much? Did I not give Simon enough in bed?

Why wasn't I enough?

"You can't help me here?" Simon barks at me, breaking my train of thought.

I look at him, meeting the angry gaze of the man I'd loved my whole adult life. But when I look at him, it is as if I don't know him. His brown eyes don't make my heart skip a beat or my skin break out in gooseflesh. He isn't the dorky, computer-obsessed guy I fell for so long ago. Now he's the man who slept with our nanny in our bed. I will never get that out of my head for the rest of my life.

I slowly shake my head. "I stopped helping you the moment you decided you were leaving."

He growls something incoherent as he throws everything back into the box and then loads the mess into the truck. Kaia starts toward me, but I cut her a look, and she pauses midstride. I know I suffer from really bad resting-bitch face, but when I actually want to turn it on, my expression can be brutal.

"I'm really sorry, Vera," Kaia squeaks.

I don't say a damned thing. She worked for us for six years. She had been one of my best friends. I know that's where

I messed up. I trusted her completely. I let her into my home life more than I should have. Yeah, she was the boys' nanny, but there was no need for her to move in with us when she broke up with her boyfriend. At least I thought she'd broken up with her boyfriend. Turns out that was part of the lie she and Simon had come up with. How did I miss the looks they shared? The intimate touches... All of it. I missed every single sign. Was it because I was naïve, or did I not care? That part has me confused. How could they have had a relationship for over a year, and I never suspected anything?

How did I allow something happening under my own nose to ruin my family?

To hurt my boys?

I hold my breath and look down at Louis and Elliot. The twins are holding on to me like I am a life preserver. Did they know before I did? I knew Charlie couldn't have...not the way he is acting. But the twins are so quiet and always keep to themselves. Had they seen something and just didn't know how to tell me? Shaking my head, I know it doesn't matter. All that matters is that I would never leave them. Never.

Simon slams the truck door and looks back at us. When his gaze meets mine, I lift my chin and fight back tears. This is it. He is leaving. He is really leaving us. And he is going with her.

"We have that appointment on Friday," he calls.

Our mediation.

"Yeah, I know."

"Okay," he says. He walks toward us and bends down on one knee. Reaching out, he takes the boys' hands and laces his fingers with theirs. "When my weekends start, we'll go to a game or something, okay?"

Neither Elliot nor Louis says anything. They just stare at him as they cling to my hands and lean into me. They look terrified, and it guts me. When a tear slides down my cheek, I rub my face against my shoulder so I can wipe the tears without letting go of the twins. I have been through a lot of stuff in my life, but this is by far the hardest.

"I do love you two. Honestly. I love Charlie, guys... I love you all."

Their silence clearly pisses Simon off. Glancing up at me, he gives me a look of distress, but I am not helping him. I can't. No matter how much I want to fix this for the boys, I know I can't. This is all Simon's decision.

"Can you talk to them?" he begs me.

I shrug. "I'll talk to Charlie about respecting you, but that's it. I won't make them talk to you."

"Yeah, thanks a lot," he says slowly as he stands. He shakes his head. "They're playing off you."

"They are not," I insist, my chin inching up. "I have been more than civil through all of this. Their anger, their hurt... All of this is brought on by you."

"Whatever. I was always here for them, while all you did was work. And now they don't want to—"

"Simon," I snap. "This all can be discussed in mediation. Until then, do not talk about me that way. You didn't have a problem with me until you did what you did with her. Which is fine. It's over. But don't disrespect me, especially when I have no intention of doing that to you."

"Always with a stick straight up your ass," he mutters as he turns briskly, heading for the truck. I look down so I don't have to watch him drive away.

Louis is watching me. I give him a weak smile, and his eyes start to fill with tears. "Will we be okay, Mom?"

I look into his sweet brown eyes. "Of course, honey. We're gonna be great."

"You promise?" Elliot chimes in.

I nod vigorously. "Yes, babe, it's all good. Promise."

"Charlie is really mad," Elliot informs me.

"I know." I reassure him, "He'll be okay. It's just gonna take some time to adjust."

Louis rubs at the tears on his cheeks. "But we'll always have each other, right?"

I smile. "Yes, hon. Me, you, Elliot, and Charlie. Forever."

They both seem satisfied with that. I look back toward Simon's truck. I close my eyes and hold my breath. I just don't understand. I really don't, and this is killing me. I don't like failing. Not in the slightest, but this... This whole situation is one big fail.

Louis leans his head on my arm, and when Elliot follows, my heart soars. But when they squeeze my hand three times, my smile disappears and the tears return.

Three squeezes: I love you.

Squeezing their hands back, I lead us back into the house.

I might have lost my husband.

But I'll never lose my boys.

# LINCOLN

Clapping my hands loudly, I let out my signature child-call, which sounds like equal parts owl and banshee. That refocuses four pairs of eyes on me. Grinning at their faces, I move my pointer along the dry-erase board and point at Max.

"To win the tutu, what letter is missing from the word *sentence*?" I ask.

I emphasize each letter, hoping my enunciation will help her, but Max is the most gifted of the Ellenton children. She doesn't need any hints, and in fact, because she is so smart, I challenge her the most.

"All the *E*s."

I throw the tutu in the air, glitter flying from it as I let out a roar of excitement. "That is correct!"

The kids giggle, and I put the tutu around my waist. It goes great with my feather boa and my fake diamond earrings.

"Put your crown back on!" Minnie, the youngest of the girls, hollers.

I steady it on my head, completing my beautiful outfit.

"It's tea time," Maven informs us.

"It is. Let's blow this popsicle stand and head to the kitchen." I throw my pointer down, and the girls run out of the schoolroom. Except May. She is my buddy and always waits for me.

"Lincoln, can you help me with my paragraphs? I hate that I missed that question on the test. I should have aced it."

I grin down at her. Her blue eyes sparkle as I wrap my arm around her shoulders. "Of course. We'll work some extra stuff in after tea time, okay?"

She beams up at me. "Thanks."

"Anytime."

Just as we cut through the foyer, the door opens and the boys spill in.

"Maverick! Matthew!" I call. "Go get that smelly stuff off and get in the schoolroom. You owe me essays on the difference between baseball and cricket. I want them done before dinner."

They fly by me.

"Nice tutu!" Maverick yells.

"Goes great with your crown," Matthew teases.

I laugh as they run up the stairs, their stench going with them. They slam the doors, and I shake my head. Six years ago, when I started with this family, the boys were all over me. And little. Now they are both teenagers, growing into their own, and if I am honest, I don't like it. I don't like that any of the kids are growing up. They are all getting older, and I worry that soon they won't need me anymore.

I still have time, though.

I figure at least another ten years since the girls are still under ten.

I sit down at my spot at the tea table in the kitchen. Maven pours me a heavy glass of sweet tea. The girls mirror me in their tutus and crowns, and we continue our tea party. After taking my phone out, I snap a few pictures and send them to Mike and Sharron, the kids' parents. They respond with emojis, which makes me smile.

"How's your sister?" Maven asks as she hands me a cookie.

"She's good. The baby should be here in a couple months."

"Will we get to go see it?" Minnie asks.

I nod. "Of course. We'll take a field trip, duh!"

The girls giggle as we eat our cookies and drink our tea. I grew up the youngest of six and the only boy. I played with more dolls and dressed up for tea parties more than any red-blooded man would care to admit. But in a way, it helped me. I was a rough, tough lacrosse player, but because of my sisters, I knew when to be gentle. I went to college on a lacrosse scholarship, but I wasn't naïve enough to think I could go pro, so I studied early childhood education.

I thought teaching would be everything I wanted. But during my senior year, before I could even complete my certification, I took a job as a nanny for extra money. I thought it would be all easy shit, but I realized I was not only working, I was a part of the children's lives. They loved me, and I loved them. When Rob, the eight-year-old, called me his manny, it stuck. I finished school and got my degree, but I didn't pursue teaching. I stayed deep in the manny game, and I am killing it.

Offers from families came daily, but I am loyal and stay with my family until I'm not needed anymore. The Ellenton family is my third and longest stint. When I say they are my second family, I'm not kidding. They wait for me to finish dinner with my biological family on the holidays so I can join them for theirs. Sharron and my mom are friends, and my dad loves the boys. We're close, and I love them. All of them.

"Lincoln, can I have another cookie?" Minnie asks, which makes me raise my brow.

"How many have you had?"

"Three," she says innocently.

"Might as well take a fourth to make your total..." I wait.

"Even!" they say in unison.

"That's right!" I cheer, throwing my hands in the air.

Man, I love my job.

◆ ◆ ◆ ◆

As I clean up the kitchen, I poke my head into the family room. All the kids are on the couch watching a movie. I check the time on the casserole right as the front door opens. Mike and Sharron work in the city and ride the train back to our little suburb.

"Hey, guys," I say, taking the casserole out of the oven and setting it on the counter. "How was work?"

Sharron smiles. "Work."

Mike nods as they go to the living room to say hi to the kids. "Hey, Linc, can you stay for dinner? Maybe after, for a drink?"

I look away from the cabinet, a stack of plates in my hand. His tone is worrisome, but I nod nonetheless. I don't have plans anyway. It isn't like I am dating anyone at the moment. "Sure."

"Great."

When he doesn't say anything more, a certain sense of dread settles in my stomach. Despite my vague sense of worry, dinner is full of laughs and storytelling. The adults retreat to the kitchen for an after-dinner whiskey while the kids go upstairs to get ready for bed. That nervous feeling returns once I'm alone with Mike and Sharron. I don't like the way they seem to avoid looking me in the eye, and I sure as hell don't like the feeling of guilt that swims in my chest. Did I do something wrong? Was I too hard on the boys about the essays they half-assed? *Shit.*

"So, Linc, we have some bittersweet news."

I look from my glass to Mike. "Oh?"

"Yeah." He threads his fingers with Sharron's before they both finally look at me. "I got that job in Germany."

My stomach sinks.

"You did." I barely get the words out, but I recover well. I knew he was applying—he told me about it months ago. But when I didn't hear anything else, I assumed he hadn't gotten it. "That's great. Congratulations. I know you wanted this."

"I did. Thank you."

"How much time do I have to get ready for the move?" I laugh. I'm not ready to move, especially with my sister having a baby and everything, but this is my career. I wouldn't leave the family hanging. I'd agreed I would go with them when he said he was applying.

But when he looks back down, my dread returns.

"That's the thing, Linc. We aren't going to take you with us."

I feel like someone has knocked the air out of me. "Oh."

"I'm not going to work since he'll be making more money than we both make now," Sharron says. "They're paying for our housing, which means I can stay home and be with the kids. Homeschool them the way I wanted—not that you haven't done an amazing job. Please don't think I mean it that way," she adds in a rush.

I reach over and take her free hand with mine. "I'd never think that," I say, my heart pounding in my chest. "It's so great

17

for you."

"It is," she says, and then she starts crying. "We are torn over this decision—"

"But it's the best for us." Mike's voice is steady, but his expression is sad.

"No, I completely understand," I agree, letting out a long breath. "Just surprised."

"We know. We're so sorry."

"Don't be," I urge, squeezing her hand. "I get it. You guys really wanted this job."

"We did, but we're so sad to lose you," Sharron says, wiping her face. "You've been a part of this family for so long."

I quirk my brows. "And a move across the world won't change that."

Mike cups my shoulder, squeezing it hard. "We're giving you six months' pay up front to help until you find another family. We will write the best recommendations."

I smile gratefully. "I appreciate that. So you'll be moving soon?"

"The end of the month."

Another punch to the gut. "Wow. Damn."

"Yeah. It's sudden, but they took so long to decide who they wanted, they want us there quickly. They're paying for everything and giving us a moving bonus." Mike grins. "That we're handing to you."

"You don't have to," I insist, even though I really can use the cushion until I find another family.

"No, we are. It's the least we can do. It's so hard to let you go."

And it is going to be hard for me to let them go.

# CHAPTER TWO

## LINCOLN

I reach for the glass that my buddy's wife, Riana, holds out to me, and I smile. "Thanks for having me over."

I lean back in my chair, so full from the amazing dinner she cooked. We usually have dinner every Thursday night when Phillip is in town, but lately, he has been traveling a lot, and Riana is helping her sister through a nasty divorce. It is nice to be back with them. I've missed them.

Phillip claps my shoulder. "You're always welcome. Wish we could have had you over sooner. With everything going on and my travel schedule, it's been nuts."

"I know, man. No big."

"How are you doing since your family moved?" Riana asks.

I shrug. Phillip and I have talked about it, but I guess he hasn't told Riana.

"It sucks, but they gave me a six-month severance, so I'm okay."

"Yeah, but you miss them."

I nod. "I do. Jenny doesn't want me to get another family."

Phillip gives me a look. "I don't always say this, but I agree with your sister."

I shoot him an incredulous look. "No, no you can't."

He laughs. "Really, I think you should go into the field for real. You're a wonderful teacher."

"Thanks," I say with a shrug. "But I love the freedom of homeschooling and taking care of kids."

"What about teaching at a private school?"

I nod. "I don't know. I need to figure it out. My mom and sisters want to talk to me."

"Ew." Phillip groans.

I laugh at that. Phillip knows all about my gossiping family; he dated Vanessa, one of my older sisters. It was a quick hookup that fizzled just as fast, but at the end of it, he met Riana. The night Vanessa broke up with him, Riana was their waitress. Funny how things like that happen.

"Either way," he says. "You gotta do what makes you happy."

"It's hard, ya know? I thought I had at least ten more years with them."

"That's why taking care of families sucks," Phillip says.

Riana's phone rings. She smiles in apology and heads to the kitchen.

"I've been looking at families," I say. "I just haven't been impressed by anyone."

Phillip laughs. "You know you'll never find another one like the Ellentons."

"I know. Man, I had it so good there."

We share a laugh. I hear Riana's voice rising in the kitchen.

Phillip says, "You did have it good, but now it's time to

grow up and be a big boy. Get a serious job."

I nod.

"I can talk to my mom. She has some pull over at Liberty Hall."

Phillip and I both went to the local private school; that's where we met. It is a nice enough school, but man, do I really want that? A nine-to-five? I've had such freedom the last six years. I can do whatever I want as long as the kids are cared for. I have to admit that most of the time being a manny feels more like being a brother than actually having a job. But like Phillip said, maybe it is time for me to put my big-boy pants on.

"You've got to be kidding me!" Riana's face is red as she comes toward us. "That was Vera."

Phillip pinches the bridge of his nose. "What now?"

"Another nanny quit."

His face scrunches up. "She just hired this one last week!"

"The boys covered the entrance to the kitchen with clear packing tape. She didn't see it and ran right into it."

Phillip starts laughing, and I can't help joining in until Riana silences us with a look.

"The girl freaked out so bad! She got wrapped up in the tape. They had to cut the tape out of her hair, and it pulled some of her eyelashes out. She was carrying a hot bowl of soup, and it burned her thighs. Still wanna laugh?"

Our laughter dies off as Riana shakes her head. "She wants to sue. So of course, Vera is freaking out."

"Well that sucks," Phillip adds.

I nod. "The boys did that? They are great kids, really well-behaved last time I saw them."

Riana falls into a chair and covers her face. "They are honestly the best kids in the world, but when my sister's fuckhead husband left, they went crazy."

"Especially Charlie, the oldest. He's taking it hard," Phillip says.

I lean back in my chair. "He probably thinks if he chases off the nannies, his dad will come back."

Riana looks over at me, and I see the tears in her eyes. "Exactly. He hates school; he hates the nannies. That isn't Charlie. He is such a good kid. I hate what Simon has done to my sister and those boys."

"We all do, baby," Phillip says, getting up and going to her. He wraps his arms around her neck and kisses her temple. "Don't worry, Vera is so strong."

"She's at her wit's end, though. This is the ninth nanny that has quit." Riana runs her hands down her face, wiping away her tears. "All Vera has is us, and it's killing me."

Nine nannies? Jesus Christ, what were those kids doing?

"I know, baby. We'll figure it out. Don't get yourself so upset."

"It's hard not to," she says softly. "I don't want to live with them. I want to live here and grow our family."

"It's fine, Riana. Calm down," Phillip says, and then he laughs. "Sorry, man, she's emotional as shit."

I wave him off. "Hey, I know how it is to have sisters, especially when they're pregnant. You want to be there for them no matter what, so it's hard when they hurt."

"Exactly," Riana says, holding her hand out to me. "I tell him he doesn't know what it's like to have siblings."

"Excuse me for having parents that got it right the first time."

While Phillip and I laugh about that, Riana looks distressed.

"Charlie isn't doing well in school either, and if he doesn't bring his grades back up, they'll cut him from club sports. Shit, her stress is stressing me out."

"Riana—"

"No, I'm sorry to ruin the night. I'm going to head over there."

But Phillip won't let her get up. "Why?"

"She needs me."

"She does not. She can look at the endless ads and find someone else."

"I know, but she's upset. I should be there."

"She can handle it. I swear it. You baby her, but you're the younger sister," he says, squeezing her shoulders. "I get it. This sucks, and fuck Simon, but Vera is capable of standing on her own two feet. You know it pisses her off when you coddle her."

"I just hate that she is struggling so much with this. It isn't fair. She was all-in while Simon was fucking the damn nanny and anyone else he could get his hands on."

I grimace as I take a long swig of my whiskey. I don't know Vera, but I can only imagine how destructive that situation would be for all of them. Especially the kids.

Riana gives me a weak smile. "I wish there were someone who could withstand three boys. Someone who loves being a nanny because of the joy it gives them and not just the money. Maybe not a nanny, but a *manny*."

"Me?" I ask and then laugh. "Not me, right? You guys were just saying I should get a real job."

"That was before my sister needed you."

"She doesn't even know me!"

"It doesn't matter. She needs you."

"Riana, Vera said she didn't want a male nanny," Phillip protests.

"Well, that's too damn bad, because the nine females she hired didn't work, and Lincoln is the best."

When she stands up, I stand too. "I don't know, Riana. If I'm not what Vera wants..."

"She doesn't know you. She needs your help, Lincoln. I need your help. Please tell me you'll help me."

"Riana, don't put that pressure on him."

"No, seriously." She glances back at me, her eyes begging mine. "I need you to help me. I need my sister to be okay. It's been shit for so long, and she cared for me when there was no one. She put me through college. She paid for my wedding... Damn it, I need you."

Phillip looks away. "Riana, I want to help too, but—"

I hold my hand up, stopping my best friend's words. As the youngest of seven, I usually didn't get to have much say, but in this situation, I do. I have a voice. Wasn't I just saying I feel like I'm not done helping people? Now a friend is asking for my help.

And it feels so damn good to be needed again.

### VERA

"I cannot believe you!"

I know Charlie isn't listening. His head is on the kitchen island, his beanie pulled all the way down past his nose as he groans loudly.

And obnoxiously.

"How dare you think it is okay to inflict pain on someone!"

"I didn't think she'd get hurt," he says simply, not making eye contact with me.

"So then, it's okay?"

"Yes," he groans. "I don't need a nanny. I'm fourteen."

"You're a child! Your behavior proves that."

More groaning.

"You tell me that you want to have more responsibilities, to be taken seriously. But, my love, she had to cut her hair. She wants to sue me. And I had to miss even more work."

"Oh, no," he mutters.

It takes everything not to scream. I know the kids hate that I work so much—hell, I don't like it either—but it is the way I make ends meet. Before, I did it because I loved it, but now, I do it because I have to. And because I'm in competition with my fucking ex to give the boys all they want.

Pathetic, I know. But it is what it is.

If I thought I disliked him before, my anger at Simon has done nothing but get stronger. Not only is he forcing me to keep the boys in a school they do not care for, he suggested I should pay half. Because his *wife* is now pregnant. If it isn't enough that I am hurting because my boys and I weren't enough for him, the fact that he has moved on while I've done nothing but clean up the mess he left behind and try to make a life for us is making me miserable.

Which seems to be our new normal.

Now, if only my son would cooperate, it could be a tad easier.

"I didn't want you to miss work, Ma. I didn't think it would be this bad."

"Well, it is," I snap back at him as I scrub a glass violently. "And to bring your brothers into this... Charlie, you are the example."

"Didn't sign up for that. I actually didn't sign up for any of this, but here I am."

Whipping around, I throw my sponge in the sink. "And what does that mean?"

"It means I didn't ask for my family to split up, to have nannies brought in to be the only ones to care for us. I want my dad to care for me. I want my mom to be there, more than to just tuck us into bed. I don't want some other person."

"Well, that's too damn bad, because we weren't given that option," I yell, and I hate that I'm yelling, but damn it, what in the hell am I going to do? These boys have run off more nannies than most kids have in an entire childhood, and I know darn well that Riana does not want to help me anymore. She has her own life. I can't blame her. "My love, do you think I want it this way? I loved our life with your father. I loved that we had it all figured out. But all that is in the past, Charlie. This is our reality now, and we're all trying to figure it out. But damn it, I need you to stop working against me. Work with me. You're not hurting anyone but me, my love. Don't you see that?"

His eyes, those beautiful chocolate-brown eyes, meet mine. I can see them welling up, and the sight sends daggers to my heart. I understand his pain; I feel it too, but I need some give here. I don't want to put this pressure on him. I want him to focus on school and enjoy being a teenager, but I don't know how else to express how much I need him to cool it. "You were never like this before, Charlie. Please. Help me."

"No, you didn't."

I drop my hands to my thighs, confused. "What?"

"You didn't love your life with him," he says slowly. He stands from the kitchen counter and pushes his beanie up his head. "You didn't even love *him*. You love your work, and sometimes I think it even comes before us."

"Charlie! You know that's not true!"

"Not all the time. I said sometimes. You're always in the front row at our games, cheering us on. I know you love us and that you think you loved your life when Dad was here, but you never loved him."

"Yes—"

"I think I saw you two kiss maybe ten times in my life."

"Charlie—"

"And you never had sex."

"For the love of Christ! Charlie!"

He goes on, his eyes so intently on mine. So full of hurt and yearning. Jesus, what should I say here?

"I think I caught my friends' parents having sex more times than I ever saw you two hold hands. You think you hid all the fighting, but you didn't. I heard you. I don't know what happened because it wasn't always that way. It all happened sometime after you changed jobs, and I don't think you realized it happened, Mom, but it did. You didn't notice, but we did."

Just like when Simon told me he was leaving, my heart shatters in my chest as tears rush to my eyes. Looking down at the ground, I bring in a deep breath and try to swallow back my sob. Blinking away my tears, I look up at my oldest. "I am so sorry for all of that. I am so sorry I couldn't keep him here, but Charlie, I need you—"

Before I can even finish, he turns and starts out of the kitchen. I follow, yelling at his back. "I need you to realize I need your help! You are the man of this house. We need to be a team—"

"I don't want to be on your team!" he shouts and turns toward me, tears rolling down his cheeks. "I want our lives back, but we weren't enough!"

I snatch Charlie's shirt and tug him close to me. He widens his eyes. "You listen to me right now, Charlie Tomas." I strain to control the tears rolling down my cheeks. "You are enough, Elliot is enough, Louis is enough, and damn it, I am enough! He isn't! He doesn't get to dictate our future. We do—"

Pushing my hands away, he shakes his head. "If we were enough, he wouldn't have left us."

Oh, my God, this is the perfect moment for me to say he is a cheating bastard, but I promised myself I would never do that. I would never run his name through the mud and turn my children against him. At the end of the day, Simon is a wonderful father but a shit husband. Which is why I never would have left him. I just never thought he'd leave me.

Turning from me, Charlie takes the steps two at a time. Before I can say anything else, I see Louis and Elliot at the top of the stairs, watching me with tears in their eyes, mirroring each other with their expressive faces. When they run toward Charlie's room, I let my shoulders sink and my head fall forward.

I remember when we found out I was having identical twin boys; we were so damn excited. Charlie was five and wanted a little brother or sister. When we told him it was two, he cried in eagerness. Simon and I had just gotten married a few weeks before we found out, and we were finally going to be one big beautiful family. Gosh, at the sweet and tender age of twenty-one, I thought I had it all and that the twins would be our new start.

Jesus, come to think of it, I've had more new starts than I care to admit.

Maybe Charlie is right.

Not that he and the twins aren't enough. They are everything and then some.

But that I'm not enough.

Never was.

♦ ♦ ♦ ♦

I run my hand through my hair and inhale and exhale deeply before my next sip of wine. I haven't left the island since my fight with Charlie. Looking at the computer screen, I search through each of the nannies on the site. None of them are qualified enough for my kids. They're either too young and not able to drive or too old and would probably die of a heart attack when my kids do whatever they are gonna do to them. I need someone strong, someone able to handle three rough, tough, hurting boys.

God, I hate that they are hurting.

Leaning back in my chair, I shut my computer and shake my head. I'm going to have to take the day off tomorrow. My boss, Richard, will not appreciate that, but what else can I do?

*Damn it.*

Just before I dial his number, I hear my name.

"Vera."

It's Riana.

I almost cry out in joy. I didn't want to ask her to come; she's done enough. But being the great sister she is, she is here. I stand up, throw back the rest of my wine, and put my glass in the sink. "I'm in the kitchen."

I hear the sounds of the boys running down the stairs and then their chatter as Riana scolds them. "Really? Duct tape?"

"She was awful," Charlie says simply.

"She didn't like loud noises," Elliot adds.

"And we're loud," Louis says.

The trill of her laughter mixed with Phillip's runs down my spine as I head toward the living room. I don't want them to feed into the boys' madness, but that's their right as their aunt and uncle, I guess. Turning the corner, I try to smile, but I'm caught off guard when a pair of light-gray eyes meet mine.

And they do not belong to my sister or brother-in-law.

Holy. Shit. Who the hell is this?

I'm stunned and blinking as I take in the man. I always thought Phillip was tall, but this guy towers over him. His shoulders are broad but not too broad—the perfect size. His waist is trim and his legs so darn long. His dark hair is a mess at the top but nicely shaved up the sides. He wears a simple pair of jeans with a button-down flannel that looks tight at his shoulders. I have never been attracted to someone who wears flannel. Simon normally wore suits, or dress shirts with pressed jeans, yet I am drooling over this guy in flannel.

But that isn't what has my gut in knots. No. It's his eyes—such a light gray, they remind me of beautiful storm clouds. I feel lost in them as we look at each other. Blinking, I take in the sweet freckles on his face, which remind me of Elliot's. Those freckles are the only thing that help me tell the boys apart, but on this man, they aren't adorable; they are sexy. And holy shit, he has a beard. It's nicely trimmed, giving him a distinguished look.

A fucking sexy look.

*Jesus.*

It's hard to tear my gaze from his. He's drinking me in. I feel his stare burn all over my skin. As he turns his gaze down my face to my neck, he stops. What the hell? Following where his eyes are aimed, I realize I have a few too many buttons undone. Heat explodes along my chest as I hurriedly fasten up my blouse so there is a lot less of me exposed. Looking up to see if anyone notices, I see him watching me, those light eyes wanting more.

Who the hell is this guy?

And why am I hot?

I look to my sister, my eyes wide. She looks back at me, and I don't miss the little grin that pulls at her lips.

"I am here to rescue all of you." The man smiles.

"Hey! Linc! What's up?" says Charlie.

He holds out his hand to shake Charlie's.

"Been on the field?" Charlie asks.

Linc—*and what kind of name is "Linc"?*—laughs. "No, man. I've been so busy."

"That sucks!"

"It's the life of an adult." Linc laughs again, and I find myself smiling. His laugh is deep and throaty.

Jesus, he's pretty. I want to rub myself on him. *Ack.* What the hell is wrong with me?

Clearing my throat, I ask, "I take it you two know each other?"

Everyone looks at me, but Phillip's smile grabs my attention. "This is my buddy, Lincoln Scott. We went to school together. The boys have met him a few times."

"Oh," I say simply. I don't miss the way that Lincoln is looking at me. I may have been out of the game for a very long time, but I know when a man likes what he sees. Unfortunately, I know that because I watched my husband look at other women.

He steps toward me, and I find I'm holding my breath. He holds out his hand, his eyes dancing with mine. "Hi. I'm Lincoln."

"Oh." I take his hand with every intention to shake it quickly and be done with it, but apparently he has a different plan. Within seconds, his hand swallows mine and holds it tightly as his eyes burn into mine. Heat runs up my arms, my breath catches, and I swear I feel like I am the one who ran into duct tape and fell to my death.

I blink. He grins.

Riana claps her hands together. "So, I found your

replacement for a nanny."

The spell broken, I pull my hand from his quickly, begging my body to behave. I try to ignore Hotty McHot and pull my brows up. "What? How?"

She just grins, and even with the shit day I've had, I can't help but smile. She is glowing and beautiful with her dark-blond bob and thick yellow glasses. I've always admired her style. I'm just plain, but she's always been intriguing. When I was pregnant, I looked like a cow, but she is stunning. I can't wait to meet my little niece. I envy Riana, and while I know it's wrong, I hope I always envy her. Because that would mean she'd always be happy. I want that for her. Always.

"The family this person was with just moved three months ago," she says. "He comes with great credentials, and we know him really well."

My brows come together in confusion. "Excuse me. *Him?*"

"Yeah. Lincoln," she says, hooking her thumb to him. "The manny."

My furrow digs deeper into my forehead, but I don't miss the pure excitement on my children's faces.

"No way!" Charlie exclaims.

I point to the guy I was just ogling ten seconds ago and almost had a coronary touching. "Him?"

Lincoln's grin pulls at his lips. "Me."

I fumble on my words. "But, but...you're a man."

Everyone laughs except me.

"Good observation. I am."

Oh, a smartass. Wonderful.

Elliot is hopping on his heels. "Mom, this would be so cool. Lincoln is so much fun."

I don't want fun. I want someone who can throw the hammer down! Someone to keep them alive and get them from point A to point B. Fun is the last thing I need. And a man to take care of my children? That just isn't what I want. I want someone nurturing—nice but hard—and someone who doesn't awaken my wild loins.

*My wild loins! Wow.*

Leaning toward me, Phillip whispers, "Change your face before Riana starts yelling."

I didn't even realize I was making a face until I glance back at Riana. She is, of course, glaring and very annoyed. I clear my throat and ask, "Can I talk to you in the kitchen?"

She squints before leaning down to kiss Louis's head. "Yeah, come on."

I turn and notice Lincoln watching me. His eyes are intent on mine, his gray gaze so deep I swear it's as if he is challenging me. As if he is daring me not to hire him! I don't know this man from Adam, so why the hell would I hire him? He doesn't know what I want to talk to my sister about. Why do I care about what he thinks of me? Why do I like the way his lips quirk?

Oh, yeah, he's trouble.

My annoyance runs deep as we reach the kitchen. I shake my head as I move around the island, and I look up to see Riana crossing her arms across her chest, gently resting them on her growing stomach.

"Riana—"

"What? He's great," she says, cutting me off. "Honestly,

Vera, he is amazing. He was with his last family for six years, and they love him. I had him forward all his credentials and letters of recommendation to you. You won't find anyone else like him."

"Well, no, 'cause he's a man!"

"Just open your computer and read through his stuff. I don't know why the fact that he has a cock swinging between his legs matters, but for real, drop it."

It matters because I wouldn't mind seeing said cock.

Unable to say that to my baby sister, I open my computer. Like she said, there are emails from Lincoln. I open each one as she comes around, reading them along with me.

Riana leans in. "He was a pillar in the Ellentons' lives. He homeschooled them, he drove them all over the place, and he was basically family. The family before that he didn't homeschool, but he did ten-hour days with them, and again, they adored him. He is a hard worker, he loves kids, and he is amazing. I mean, he's been best friends with Phillip for years."

Every file I open reveals the love and admiration the families had for Lincoln. Even some of the kids wrote letters. It is a lot to take in, but still, I am hung up on the fact that he is a man. "Riana, I don't know how I feel about a man caring for my children."

"Simon cared for them."

"He's their father."

"Phillip cares for them."

"Family," I say simply. "I don't know. It doesn't feel right."

"Well, it's gonna have to feel right. You're out of options. No one else wants to come here, and I can't do it, Vera."

I look away, biting the inside of my cheek. I know she can't, despite the fact that I would rather that happen than anything. "I am aware of that—"

"He would honestly be the best thing for them. Someone they can look up to when Simon isn't with them. They can talk to him. He'd be a buddy who doesn't take shit from them. They know him already. They get along great. Really, you need him."

"I don't need anyone but my children."

She glares. "You know what I mean. You need someone good. He is great, honestly." I look away once more, shaking my head as she goes on. "He was about to get a teaching job, but he wants to help us out."

My pride comes rearing its ugly head. "Oh, so we're a charity case?"

"No, dumbass. You're gonna pay him, and he costs more than the regular nannies you've had."

"Riana, I can't afford more."

"Which is why Phillip and I will pay the difference."

I hold her gaze. "Jesus, are we that bad you don't want to be here?"

She shakes her head. "No, not at all. But I want to be with my husband and our child when she comes. I can't raise your kids and mine."

"I wouldn't expect you to," I say softly.

"I know, but I would want to, and then I'd have to take care of you."

I scoff at that. "I don't need caring for."

She holds my gaze. "You do, but you'd never admit it." Silence falls over us, and I take her hand in mine, swallowing hard.

"Charlie said I never loved Simon," I whisper before meeting her gaze. "We got into a huge fight, and he said that I was just going through the motions, basically."

"You were," she says simply. "But if my husband cheated on me as much as yours cheated on you, I would do the same."

I scoff. "You'd have left him."

"I would have, but I don't know what it's like to have three kids with someone while just getting my feet wet at a new job. He's gone now, though."

I nod. "And this is my fresh start."

"It is," she says, squeezing my hand before our fingers lock together. "And seriously, Lincoln would be a great fit here. I wouldn't say that unless I believed it."

I swallow hard. I trust my sister with my life and my children's lives. She is all I have. All I need. But still I'm hesitant. Leaning toward her, I drop my voice to a whisper. "Does he have to look like that hot firefighter on *Chicago Fire*?"

Her face breaks into a wide smile. "You think he's hot?" she gushes, and I smack her.

"Shut it!"

She giggles before leaning back a bit to look into the living room. With a shrug, she says, "I guess I never noticed. He's always been Phillip's bestie, not the dude I wanted to do."

How the hell she hasn't noticed he is beyond hot is beyond me. I inhale hard as she giggles.

"He does have a nice ass."

"Riana!"

She laughs. "When was the last time you got laid?"

"Riana, enough!"

"He's my age, so that's not robbing the cradle. You could totally do him."

"Oh, my God, kill me now."

"Hmmm, I love this."

"You're a bitch."

"Love you too." She giggles and kisses my cheek.

I want to smack her, but I won't.

Shaking my head, I let it drop as I close my eyes. "I need help, and you're right, I can't get anyone in here by tomorrow."

"No, and he's ready to start now."

It is almost too easy, but then...is it?

"I'm pretty sure I can ask him to be ugly. He'd do it for me."

I squeeze my eyes shut. "Riana."

"Or you can just jump his bones and bang it out. He wouldn't turn you down. You're way too hot."

"For the love of God," I mutter, covering my face. "Why in the hell did I say anything?"

"Because at this point, that is the only reason you wouldn't hire him," she says, smacking my butt playfully. "Too bad that excuse won't work for me, because he's hired."

"You can't hire him. This is my home."

"I don't care! You need him, so get on board! And if you find yourself naked with him, don't ruin it." She wiggles her brows at me before she yells, "Hey, Linc! Come in here, please."

"As if, Riana."

She snorts. "Hey, like I said, you need someone to care for the boys, and if he can care for you, he's worth every penny in my book. I'll even send him a bigger fruit basket than I already send for Christmas."

"You're impossible!"

Her laughter continues as Lincoln enters the room, and I swear the air rushes out of me. He's so damn big, so thick, and Jesus, he's my new nanny.

Oh, wait, I'm sorry...my new *manny*.

# CHAPTER THREE

### LINCOLN

"How old is she?"

Phillip looks over at me as he jerks to the left with a controller in his hand. He has always been awful at video games, but I don't think the boys mind. "Who?"

"Riana's sister."

"Vera? Oh, she's three years older than us."

That would only make her thirty-one.

I lean back on the couch, trying to catch a glance of her. She doesn't look like a mom that should have a kid Charlie's age. I probably shouldn't say this about my new boss, but fuck, she's hot. I mean, not kind of hot either. Full-blown naughty-kitten sexy. I don't know many moms who wear slacks and a nice blouse at six o'clock in the evening and look that damn good. Her long dark hair hangs to her breasts...which I might add are mouthwatering. Heavy and round on her curvy body. She isn't fat by far, but she isn't skinny either. Her hips are wide, and that ass is of another world. She is rocking that hourglass frame like a pro, and I want nothing more than to run my hands up and over those curves. How in the hell am I supposed to work for her?

"But Charlie is like—"

"Fourteen, almost fifteen," he says, leaning the other way. "She had him when she was sixteen."

That is surprising to me for some reason, but I don't know why. Sage, my oldest sister, had her first kid when she was sixteen, so it isn't as though I've never met a young mom. I'm intrigued. I want to know more.

"So what happened to the husband?" I ask in a low voice since the boys are sitting with us.

"Left her for the nanny," Phillip whispers back, shaking his head.

"Yeah, I guessed that," I say with a nod.

"Yup, he is a douche. Vera deserves better."

"Yeah."

"But the boys are great, when they aren't pranking nannies."

Elliot heard that and grins back at us. "They were awful."

"Really, they were," Louis says then.

Charlie sits up straighter and shrugs. "We don't need anyone to care for us. We have a mom and a dad."

"Well, buddy, I don't know if you forgot, but you've also always had a nanny," Phillip reminds him.

Charlie shrugs. "To help. Mom wants to replace Dad."

"That's not true," Phillip says, letting his controller fall after he pauses the game.

Charlie looks back at him, his brows pulled together.

"Your mom needs help, just like the nannies helped before," says Phillip. "Don't put that blame on your mom. She has too much going on as it is."

"I'm not."

"With what you just said, it sounds like you are."

He shrugs. "I just want my dad back."

"Yeah, I wanted mine, buddy, but it doesn't matter what we want. That's the hand we're dealt. Be thankful you have a mom who loves you and actually cares. Plus one super-cool uncle and an all-right aunt," Phillip says, squeezing Charlie's shoulder.

I didn't think the boys knew Phillip's upbringing, but by the dark looks on their faces, I guess I am wrong. Phillip didn't have it easy growing up. When his dad left, his mom couldn't get her shit together, and it was three months before his dad found out Phillip was going without food—so he filed for custody.

Charlie sends him a strained smile. "You're right, I'm sorry."

"Don't apologize to me. Be easy on your mom."

Charlie turns to leave, and Phillip looks to me, shaking his head. "He's a good kid, but this divorce has fucked him up," he whispers.

I nod. "Understandable."

"I hate that dude," he mutters as he leans back. "I just want Vera to be happy."

"Is she not?"

Phillip scoffs. "No. She's going through the motions, but then she's always been like that. I don't think that girl has ever lived."

"Why do you say that?"

"She has always taken care of everyone else. Never took

care of herself. Then while the twins were younger, she worked her ass off to get through school. She's been grinding since she was sixteen, never taking a moment for herself." He looks over at me, his voice low. "Only mistake she made was marrying some dude who couldn't keep it in his pants."

"Really?" I ask in a low voice, hopeful the boys don't hear us.

"Yup. But he is the father of her children, so she never left," he says with a shrug. "Either way, she puts on a hard face and acts tough, but she's really great."

"I didn't think otherwise."

He sends me a grin just as Riana yells, "Hey, Lincoln! Come in here, please."

I am up before she even finishes her sentence. I pause, though, when Phillip laughs.

"Eager, huh?"

"Shut up," I throw back to him before heading toward the kitchen. The house is big, nicely done, and very homey. It has a farmhouse feel, and it isn't what I would have expected from someone who looks like Vera. I figured she'd have some posh pad with boys who didn't move, but I know darn well those boys move. They are lacrosse players. My kind of guys.

Entering the kitchen, I find Riana snickering as Vera rolls her eyes, but when she sees me, she sits up straighter.

And I direct my eyes straight to her chest.

Again.

First time wasn't my fault—her shirt was unbuttoned— but this time, totally a pig move on my part.

Inhaling hard, I smack my hands together, forcing myself

to look at Riana. "So, am I hired?"

Riana just grins. "Duh—"

"I do have questions," Vera says then, and I glance back to her, captured by her brown gaze. Her eyes are such a deep brown with flakes of gold in them. Her lips are plush and thick while her chin has a little dip in it. Looking away to the computer, she says, "Your last family moved?"

"They did," I say and then clear my throat. "I was supposed to go with them, but Sharron, the mom, decided to stay home with them."

She slowly nods. "And you would have moved to Germany with them? Don't you have family here?"

"I would have. I love those kids, and I wanted to be there for them. My family does live here, along with Phillip, but I wouldn't have been gone forever."

She looks up at me. "That's very loyal."

I shrug. "Guess I'm a loyal guy."

"You were full-time for them?"

I nod.

She continues. "Did Riana tell you that it wouldn't be full-time here?"

"Well, no, but I figured it could be," Riana adds.

Vera makes a face. "How?"

"The boys hate school. Let them be homeschooled—"

Vera shakes her head. "I can't commit to that yet. I have to talk to Simon, and the therapist still isn't sure that is the way to go yet."

I'm not sure if I should say anything, but then I'm talking. "With divorce, sometimes it isn't good to change so much.

Maybe just give it a little more time."

Vera looks at me, her eyes narrowed and her lips pressed hard together. I can see the annoyance burning in her eyes, and I'm confused by it. Does she not like me? Yet, she holds her hand out to me and says, "Exactly."

Riana doesn't agree with us, her face giving her away as she shakes her head. "Fine. I just think they need out of that school."

"I feel the same, but I can't do that yet," Vera says, and I can see the struggle swirling in her eyes. Her shoulders are taut, and she looks defeated. I want to wrap my arms around her, hold her, and tell her that things will be okay. Though I can't guarantee it, I want to tell her anyway. It's obvious things haven't been easy for her; nonetheless, she looks like she could take on the world. I respect what she is saying, though Riana doesn't seem to. It's hard with kids, especially when they don't know how to handle what is happening, which I suspect is what is going on with Vera's boys.

When she looks at me once more, her dark eyes hold mine as she says, "So it wouldn't be full-time."

The way she says it, along with her eyes, I feel like she is hoping I'll turn her down, but I can't.

"That's okay." I'm not sure why I say that because it isn't okay. I need a full-time position.

But I want to help her.

Her eyes don't leave mine, and when her tongue moves across her lips, I swallow hard.

"Okay," she says almost in a whisper. "I leave in the morning at seven for work, but the boys don't need to be at school until eight. They are driven to school and picked up at three. The last nanny would bring them home so they could get their stuff together for club. They play lacrosse for the Knights over—"

"The boys I cared for played for the Knights. I know where they are."

"Oh," she says, her lashes kissing her cheeks before she inhales deeply, her chest moving with the motion. She looks away, but I can't bring myself to do the same. I am captivated by her. It's been a while since I've wanted a woman so completely, and man, I want Vera.

Which is wrong. So damn wrong.

She is about to be my boss.

Swallowing hard, I look away, but not far enough away because Riana's gaze catches mine, a little grin on her face as her eyes start to widen. My brows pull together as I mouth, *what*, and she just grins.

*You like her*, she mouths back. *She's so hot, right?*

I can't help it. I laugh a bit, which brings Vera's attention to mine, so of course, I start coughing. "Sorry. Something in my throat."

She doesn't seem impressed. "I'll get home around seven on Monday, Wednesday, Friday, but on Tuesdays and Thursdays, I get home at four. So on my late days, they'll need to be fed. But on my short days, I'll meet you at practice. Things change a lot since I don't ever want to miss anything, and we're still trying to figure out things with my ex. He wants the kids from Thursday to Sunday every weekend, and that isn't okay with me, not that you need to know that."

Actually, I want to know it all.

Clearing her throat, she stands. "So if you are okay with those hours, and you still want to work for me, I'd really like to hire you right now. You can start tomorrow."

My lips curve as I lean on the island. "Can I ask a question?"

Her eyes widen a bit as she sits back down. "Of course."

"You know my rate?"

"I do. Riana and I have discussed it."

"Okay. So what else do you want me to do for you?"

Her breath catches, and I am not sure why. But when Riana tries to cover her laughter, I figure I may have come off suggestive. She clears her throat and then swallows hard before she says, "Besides getting the boys to point A and B? Being there when I'm not. I work in the city, so it will be hard for me to get here quickly."

"That's not a problem. You'll have my number. I can be here anytime you need me."

She inhales once more, her eyes burning into mine.

"Do you want me to clean? Cook?"

Her voice breaks as she asks, "You do that?"

"Yes, I can have dinner ready every night, and the house will be clean, with the boys' help."

She just blinks. "Oh."

"I usually teach the kids to cook too, if that's okay."

"That would be great."

"And I can do homework. I know you said on your short days you'll meet me, so I'll just come back here and get everything done so that it takes some of the stress off you."

She swallows hard. "I can handle my household."

Oh, the pride runs deep in her. I could see the fire in her eyes. "No doubt, but if you're paying me, might as well do it all."

Vera slowly nods before looking past me toward the living room. "Boys, do you want Lincoln to be your nanny?"

When we're met with a chorus of yeses, along with Phillip agreeing, I look back at her, smiling. She isn't, though. She looks pained as she brings her gaze back to mine. "Okay, would you like the job?"

"I would."

She actually looks surprised. "It won't be easy. The boys are hell bent on torturing anyone I hire."

I scoff. "Don't worry about the boys. I got them."

"He does," Riana says. "I think it's what the boys need. A guy to relate to."

I can see that Vera doesn't like that. Her lips purse as she looks back to me. "I really appreciate your willingness to take us on."

"The pleasure is all mine."

I may have said that a little lower than I should have, but I can't change it now. I am not usually unprofessional. I take my work very seriously, just like I plan to take this one, but I have never been attracted to my boss. I probably shouldn't take this job. Not only does it not offer the hours I need, I am way too attracted to Vera. I know the boys need me, and I feel like Vera could benefit from my help. I don't think I can do this job and keep my thoughts in line. But who said I couldn't think of her underneath me, on top of me, or bent over in front of me as I disappear over and over again inside her. Making her cry my name, her nails biting into my skin as that pouty mouth of hers covers mine. No, I can think about that all day long as long as I don't touch her.

Unless she wants me to.

No, I can't touch her.

She's newly divorced. She's my best friend's wife's sister. And damn it, she's my fucking boss.

Problem is, I can tell myself that over and over again, but it won't keep me from wanting her more than I want my next breath.

Which may become a problem.

Especially if she ever wants me.

# CHAPTER FOUR

## LINCOLN

Smiling as all the kids try to fit their faces on the screen, I laugh. "So things are good?"

Max shakes her head. "Mom is not you."

I smile. "Well, duh, but she's still amazing."

"She is, but we miss you," May says.

I nod. "I miss you guys too. Did I tell you guys that my sister named her baby after me? It's Lincoln to the second power."

They all laugh, Minnie's face the brightest. "Send us more pictures!"

"I will," I promise. "So how's Germany? Super cool?"

"It's weird," Matthew informs me, and all the kids nod. "But the pretzels are lit."

I laugh. "I heard that. Have you gotten a bratwurst yet? It's my favorite."

"Mom cooked it yesterday," Max says, but Maverick shakes his head.

"She means burned it."

That sends all of us into a fit of laughter. "Give your mom some slack. She's getting into the groove of things."

51

"We know," Maven says softly. "We do wish you were here, though."

"I know. Me too," I say on an exhale. While I do wish I were with them, I am more than excited about starting with Vera and her kids. How I got any sleep last night is beyond me. since I was tossing and turning with a hard-on that was painful. All I kept seeing were Vera's full breasts and that ass of hers. I am a little too excited to get to work today.

Not that I would tell the kids that.

"I got a new job."

All their smiles drop simultaneously.

If they didn't look so heartbroken, I'd laugh. "Guys, I have to work."

"But you're ours," May says, and then of course, she starts to cry, breaking my damn heart.

"May, calm down. You guys are still my number ones."

"But you were supposed to come here."

"Your parents didn't need me."

"So? Can't you just move here?"

I am not sure who said that, but I shake my head. "Guys, I have to work, and my family is here."

They don't like that answer, but to my surprise, it's Maven who asks, "Who are they? Are they nice?"

I smile. "You guys remember Phillip? It's his nephews."

A few of them smile as Maverick says, "Charlie, right? He plays for the Knights."

"Yup, that's him."

"Well, that's good. They're lucky to have you," Matthew says, and I smile. He isn't one to talk, so for him to say that, he meant it.

"Yeah, I'm excited to get back to work. Gives me something to do rather than miss you crazy folks."

They all smile big. "We miss you too."

I nod as I notice it's time to go in. "Okay, I gotta go. I'll send you guys pictures of Lincoln the second."

They all giggle and start screaming bye. I wave before ending the call. I exhale hard, and my heart slows a bit in my chest. I miss those kids so damn much, but I am excited for my new post. It should be interesting. That's for sure.

I throw the car door open and head up the drive toward the large colonial home. The stone house is huge and has green shutters. The porch is decorated like something off Pinterest—probably decorated by Riana. She is crafty as hell and always has me building stuff for her since Phillip doesn't know the difference between a hammer and a screwdriver. I, however, do—the perks of being the only male at home when my dad was on the road.

I laugh as I recognize a bench I made last year for Riana, realizing it was actually part of a project for Vera.

I reach the big green door and ring the doorbell. When I hear Vera's voice, I have to fight back my smile. For a stone house, the door is thin as paper.

"You guys better be ready by the time I come back up those stairs," she hollers, and I can hear her coming down the stairs. "Who in the hell comes over at six a.m. is beyond me, but the doorbell is ringing, and Charlie if it's that boy from down the road, I'm gonna wring your neck!"

The door opens, and before me stands the star of all my dreams the night before. Her eyes widen, her hands coming up to close the plush robe she wears as she blows a dark tendril out of her eye. She has just gotten out of the shower. I can see the drops of water along her neck, and my mouth goes dry, wanting desperately to lick them off her.

Swallowing hard, I smile. "Not the kid from down the road. Just your manny."

Her face flushes, her brown eyes widening even more. "I wasn't expecting you until seven."

"Yeah, Riana told me to come earlier so that we can go over everything."

She blinks. "Shit, she did tell me that." Gathering her robe more, to my dismay, she moves back to let me in. "Come in. Sorry."

"No need to apologize," I say, walking through the threshold and looking up the stairs to where the twins are. "Hey, guys."

"Hey, Linc!" Elliot says with a grin. He is standing in a towel. "Can you make that French toast you made us when we were at Riana's last time?"

"Of course," I say.

He grins before running off. Louis is fully dressed as he waves before running after his brother.

"I don't know if I have stuff for French toast," Vera says.

I shrug. "That's okay. I'll go shopping for you today. You can reimburse me."

"Oh, okay, yeah, thank you," she says before turning on her heel toward the kitchen. As wrong as it is, I watch her fine ass sway, and within seconds, I wonder how it would be to hold those thick globes in my hands. Her waist is so trim, but her ass is out of this world. She is the definition of an hourglass shape, and my mouth is watering for sure. "I haven't had a decent nanny since the one we had when I was still married, and she fucked my husband, so I'm a little rusty." She reaches for a cup and glances over to me. "Would you like a cup of coffee?"

"Please."

She clears her throat as she pours. "I think I still have the credit card I had her use," she says, more to herself, I think. But I don't care as long as she keeps talking. I love the raspiness of her voice and the way her lips move, especially when she presses a finger to her bottom lip. Looking over at me, she says, "Hopefully they don't ask for ID. I'll order you a card today."

"Sounds good," I say, swallowing hard as she hands me a cup. "Anything I need to know?"

She brings her bottom lip between her teeth, her lashes fluttering before she shrugs. "Not really. I think I covered everything last night. Make sure to write down your mileage so I can compensate you."

I nod. "Okay."

"And you have the times? It's a late night for me, so I won't be home until seven."

"Yeah, I'm good."

"Okay." She pulls a credit card and a key from her purse. "Here you are."

I take them from her, and when I look up, she is watching me. Her eyes are dark, dilated, and her lips part ever so slightly as she drags her gaze along my face. I hold her gaze as heat rushes through me. I want to touch her so fucking bad. Her skin looks so soft and luxurious. Even without the makeup she had yesterday, she is stunning. I want to tangle my fingers in her hair, and I know that's so damn bad. I shouldn't be lusting over her like this, but how can I not? She's exquisite.

She inhales and drags her gaze from mine before saying, "Well, I'm gonna go get ready. Make yourself at home."

"Will do."

She doesn't look at me as she leaves, but I can't help watching her.

That sway of her ass should be illegal.

What in the hell am I doing? I can't be ogling her like that. It's wrong, but I can't look away. *Shit.*

I haven't been with anyone in a very long time, and from the first glance, Vera has had me in knots. I don't know how or even why. I've never had this happen to me, but she just does it for me. A part of me wants to believe that she is attracted to me, but I'm pretty sure that would make me delusional. I am her employee; she wouldn't see me as anything more. I wish I had met her in different circumstances because I know I couldn't make a move if I wanted. I work for her, and that's it. The sooner I accept that, the easier it will be to keep my dirty thoughts at bay.

Because those thoughts are going to drive me mad.

I pass the time playing on my phone until I hear footsteps coming down the stairs. I stand up just as all three boys enter the kitchen. While Charlie favors Vera with his dark hair and darker eyes, the twins are lighter, which I assume is from their father. I haven't met him, nor do I want to from what I've heard. How anyone could hurt or cheat on someone like Vera is beyond me.

"Hey, Linc."

"Hey, guys," I say, slapping my hands together. "Listen, it's cereal today. I'll go shopping after I drop you guys off."

Elliot makes a face. "French toast tomorrow?"

"Absolutely."

He sends me a grin as he goes to get the cereal he wants. I lay out three bowls and then the milk, getting acquainted with everything.

"I'm glad Mom hired you," Charlie says, and I glance over at him from the fridge. "The last nannies were awful."

I smile. "I heard you guys weren't too nice to them, though."

"'Cause they sucked," Charlie answers, and I hold his gaze.

"Hey, watch your mouth, please." I can see the challenge in his eyes; he wants to fight me on it, but he just looks away. "You don't want to sound like a crappy kid. Especially when you're not."

I see the twins glance at Charlie, probably waiting for him to say something, but he doesn't. He goes back to eating. Looking back in the fridge, I write a few more things down before I ask, "How long is practice tonight?"

"Two hours," Elliot says.

"Will you be there?" Louis asks with cocoa from his Cocoa Puffs on his face.

I smile. "Yeah, I'll stay the whole time."

"Our dad usually comes on Wednesdays."

"He does?"

Looking toward the entryway of the kitchen, I feel like I'm

being knocked to my ass. In a pair of black slacks and a white sheer top, Vera puts a pair of earrings in as she eyes the boys. Her hair is halfway up, her makeup done to the nines, but all I can look at is the dip of her blouse, which shows the curve of each of her beautiful breasts.

*She's your boss. Boss. Employer. Look the other way.*

But I can't.

My mouth is dry as Charlie says, "Yeah."

"Oh," she says, looking worried as she comes toward me, her red heels sky-high as she moves past me to the coffee pot. "I'll need to call him today and let him know I hired a new nanny."

"Manny!" Elliot says.

I wink over at him.

"Yes, manny," she says dryly. I can see the hesitation on her face. She doesn't want to call her ex-husband. Can't say I blame her. "Are you guys ready to go?"

They each agree in their own ways, and I glance at Vera. She meets my gaze, and I smile. She doesn't smile back. Instead she watches me; her eyes are a bit darker as I ask, "Is there anything you need?"

"Need..." she says, her words a gasp.

I nod. "From the store?"

She blinks. "Oh, no. I'm fine. Thank you."

"Okay, you have my number, right?"

"I don't." She reaches for her phone, and we exchange numbers. "Thank you."

"Of course. I'll send you updates."

"Oh, thank you." She seems a little surprised by that. I

can't ask why, because then her gaze meets mine, and her eyes are downright sinful. There is a little tilt to them, brought out by her eye makeup. Her lashes are long and full, but it's the flakes of gold in her eyes that have me breathless. The fact that I am this attracted to her should have me running for the front door. I shouldn't chance this. I should quit and then ask her out. Though, I'm pretty sure she'd never go out with me.

She's damaged.

Doesn't take a rocket scientist to see that.

Running my tongue along my lips, I say, "Call me if you need anything."

I swear I see her take in a quick breath, and I also swear heat is radiating off her, but I'm sure it's just wishful thinking.

Nothing will ever happen between us.

No matter how much I want it to.

She looks away as she nods. "Okay."

"Cool," I say, though I'm pretty sure she won't be calling me for what I want.

Only about the job I was hired for.

## VERA

Richard's office is right next to mine, so I don't have to go far before shutting my door and heading toward my desk. I sit down and let my head fall to the desk, inhaling deeply and squeezing my eyes tightly. That meeting was awful. The look of pure disappointment in his eyes and my feelings of failure are not how I wanted to start my morning. Jesus, is he considering asking me to step down? Damn it. I work so hard for him, and yes, I've been dropping the ball. But I've been going through a lot.

But I guess in this business, personal lives don't matter.

Swallowing back my tears, I sit up and look around my posh office. I used to have a desk outside Richard's office, but now, this is all mine. The room is lined with windows, giving me an amazing view since we're on the sixty-seventh floor. But I can't even enjoy the view after the meeting. Not with the weight of the world on my chest.

I have to call Simon.

And I really don't want to.

So I won't. Not yet at least. The boys don't have to be at practice until four, so I have plenty of time before I have to call him. The anxiety of dealing with Simon is choking me at the moment. I haven't talked to him since he told the boys that Kaia is pregnant. Ugh. The thought has my stomach in knots. How he's moved on so drastically and is starting a new family just guts me. It is one thing when he was sleeping with women to get off, but this time, it isn't some meaningless fuck; it is serious.

He is starting a new family.

Swallowing hard, I wake my computer from its sleep, but before I can even open my first of a billion emails, my assistant Ronda comes over my line. "Ms. Woods, your sister is on line one."

"Thank you."

I don't have time to talk to her, but she is my sister. I would make time. Her voice rings over the line. "Hey, you."

"Hey, what are you up to?"

"I just had my doctor appointment, and baby girl is doing great!"

I smile as I click through my emails, jotting down the things I have to take care of as soon as possible. "That's wonderful. Can I call you later? I'm swamped."

"Yeah, but how'd it go this morning? Was Lincoln on time?"

"Yes, right on time," I say, and then I'm flooded by thoughts of my new "manny's" gray eyes. Lord, they are intoxicating. "He gets along with the boys well."

"Oh yeah, he's great with kids."

"Well, I know that, but he told Charlie to watch his mouth this morning, and with how he's been lately, I thought he'd pop off, but Charlie didn't say anything."

"Told you. He's gonna be great for you guys."

"Yeah, I guess," I say, though I'm not convinced. Or rather, I don't want to accept that, since all I can do is picture the man naked and on top of me. All night long I thought of him and those eyes. I swear I could feel his beard along my skin and between my legs. His eyes meeting mine as he moved his tongue along my clit, squeezing my hips in his hands.

It all seemed so real.

But it was just a dream that had me tossing and turning all night.

Shaking my head, I groan. "I just wish he wasn't so good-looking."

Her laughter fills my office. "You're insane."

"No really. Every time he looks at me, I think he's undressing me with his eyes, and then when he says certain things, they're all sexual and shit."

Her laughter continues. "They are not!"

"They are! This morning, he goes 'Do you need anything?'"

"How is that sexual?" She laughs, and I smile.

"It is as if he is saying, 'Do you need me to go between your legs?'"

"You're insane!" she says again. "You know what that means."

I roll my eyes. "What?"

"That you need to get laid, ASAP."

I scoff. "Well, he's off the table," I say quickly, and I mean it. "Not that I want to sleep with him." Now she's laughing so hard, I swear she isn't breathing. "Stop laughing!"

"You know I can see through you, right? You wouldn't talk about him so much if you didn't want to sleep with him."

"Jesus, Riana, be real! I've slept with one man my whole life. I don't just get the urge to sleep with someone after meeting them once."

"Which says a lot, big sis. You want him, and I don't blame you."

"No, I don't."

"Yes, you do," she argues. "You know it's okay to be attracted to someone."

"I know that, but not the guy who is caring for my children."

"Hey, a man is a man, and if you want him, don't deny it."

"I don't want him," I say, though I don't even believe my words. "He is just good-looking. I don't want anyone."

"Well, let me just say, you need to want someone."

"No, I don't. My divorce is just final, and he's having a baby now with her. I'm good."

"My point exactly. Get out there, meet some people. Hey!

Go out with that dude from accounting! You said he hit on you that one time."

I roll my eyes. "No way. I don't want to date."

"Who said date? I said fuck."

"Lord, Riana!"

She giggles. "Seriously. You need to get out there, bang out a few."

"No, I'm fine," I say. I try to suppress that the only person I want to bang at the moment is the manny. He came in with those eyes and looking scrumptious in a pair of nicely broken-in jeans and a thin tee, so eager to help me, and it felt so damn good. I've never had someone who just wants to make things right for me. Especially when Simon never did anything. "I don't have time anyway. Richard suggested I step down."

Riana takes in a deep breath. "Oh no."

"Yeah, so I really need to focus on getting back to where I was before everything happened."

She pauses, her voice grim as she agrees. "Yeah, but still, I think if you got back on the horse, it'd be easier. And you wouldn't have cob webs hanging in your pussy."

"Ah, fuck you," I snap at her.

She laughs. "I'm going to buy you a vibrator."

"Riana!"

"What! You need one, or three."

"Goodbye," I say before hanging up on her chortling. She is such a pain. When my phone rings again, I roll my eyes as I pick it up. "You're a pain in my ass."

"Well, hello to you too." It is Simon. Shit. I really need to have my direct-line number changed.

Closing my eyes, I cover my face. "Simon. Sorry, I thought it was Riana."

"Sure," he says, his voice making my skin crawl. "We need to discuss a few things."

"We do?"

"Yeah. Listen, can I get the boys tomorrow?"

"No," I say simply. "We've talked about this, and the judge agreed they need to be home for school."

"Then Kaia will have to pick them up."

"Why?"

"I'm leaving town tomorrow night and coming home early Saturday morning."

My blood starts to boil. "Then come get them Saturday."

"No, it's my time and Kaia wants to spend time with them."

*It's his time. It's his time. Let it be.*

Inhaling hard, I say, "Then I guess I'll have the boys ready for her on Friday at five."

He groans. "Fine. Listen, I want the boys for spring break. Kaia and I want to take them to Universal."

Universal. We were supposed to take them to Universal. "Oh, well, I don't know how I feel about that, since I wanted to take them."

He lets out a long breath. "Are we going to fight about this?"

"Am I supposed to just allow you the chance to take our children somewhere I want to take them?"

"You had plenty of time to take them; you just never stopped working."

"You didn't complain when I was bringing home money."

"Whatever. None of that matters. It's supposed to be your spring break, but we want to go before Kaia gets too big from the pregnancy."

My heart is slamming in my chest. "I'm not comfortable with that. Can we plan a trip for maybe this summer?"

"No, Kaia is due this summer."

Which means she was probably pregnant when he left me. Ignoring that sting, I shake my head. "The answer is no."

"Are you serious?"

"Yes, I want to be there when they go for the first time."

"So when will that be?"

"I don't know, but we can plan something for the future, or you can take them next spring break, since it will be yours."

"I can't believe you. You're being selfish."

"I don't feel I am. I want to experience that with my boys too."

"Whatever," he growls, but I don't care. "I'll just ask them."

"Well that's unfair," I say, leaning on my hand. "Of course they'll want to go, and I can't go right now. We can try for another time."

"Not our fault you can't get off work."

"Um, I've been getting off work left and right, trying to replace nannies with no help from you."

"Hey, I told you Kaia can keep working for you."

I laugh at that. "So you want me to have the whore you left me for nanny my children."

"Excuse me. She's their stepmother and my wife."

I bite my lip. "No."

"No what? She is."

"No, I won't give you my spring break."

"Fine. I'll take you to court over it."

"Fine. See you there."

"You're such a bitch."

The line goes dead, and my skin burns with anger. That son of a bitch. Slamming the phone down, I cover my face as I swallow back the sob that is trying to escape. I refuse to cry over that man. I've wasted too many tears on him, and I won't do it any longer. He makes me so mad I could spit. I don't know who he thinks he is, but damn it, I won't back down from him. We were planning to take the boys, but it isn't my fault he decided to leave me around that time. I am more than willing to go with him, but I won't allow him to go without me.

*Asshole.*

Turning to my computer, I click through emails, but I can't get Riana's words out of my head.

*Seriously. You need to get out there, bang out a few.*

When a knock comes at my door, I glance up and let out a heavy sigh. I just want to work and forget about my poor excuse of a love life. I don't want to talk to anyone, and I sure as hell don't want to keep thinking about Lincoln, but apparently, I won't get what I want.

"Come in."

"Hey, Vera, sorry to bother you." Dennis, the guy from accounting, enters my office. He is tall, a bit lanky, but has a nice face. He is everything that Simon is not. That alone appeals to me.

But Lincoln is the total opposite too...

*Nope, get him out of your head.*

"Dennis, no bother at all," I say with a small smile. "What can I do for you?"

He returns my smile and folds his arms across his chest like he's feeling awkward. "Richard told me to see if you need help with those RFIs."

I try not to cringe as I click to the requests for information for the quarter. I hate doing these, and now I see I am behind. "Damn RFIs." I turn my attention back to him and give a little chuckle to play it off.

He laughs, his eyes sparkling as they hold mine. He has such a nice smile. "I'm happy to help...take some of the load off."

I nod. "Thank you."

"Anytime. Just send some over," he says and then tucks his hands in his pockets. He has sweet blue eyes and no hair on his face.

Of course I notice that, since apparently beards turn me on lately. I smile, and he smiles back awkwardly.

"Yeah, so I'll go."

He turns, heading for the door, but I stop him. "Hey, Dennis, is that offer for dinner still on the table?"

When he turns, his lips part. He then stutters, "Um, yes, absolutely."

Holy crap, that was easy! I bite into my lip, uncertain whether I'm doing the right thing, but I can't shake Riana's suggestion. Plus, the boys will be gone this weekend, and it gives me time to myself. I can't work all weekend. That would be pathetic. Maybe a roll in the sheets would be nice.

Problem is, I don't really want to roll in the sheets with Dennis.

Since it isn't like I have a long line of guys asking me out, I try to beam over to him. "How about Saturday?"

He eagerly agrees and asks for my number as I try to push aside thoughts of my manny.

Gah, what a silly thing to call him.

And shit, I didn't tell Simon about him.

# CHAPTER FIVE

## LINCOLN

"You didn't have to come check on me. I know how to do my job."

From his lawn chair, Phillip laughs as he glances over at me. "I don't care about you. I came to watch my nephews."

I smile, knowing he's full of shit. "Do you do this often?"

"When I have time, thank you," he says simply.

I can't help but scoff at his lie. I know Riana wants to make sure she was right when she asked me to help. She was. I know how to care for kids, and the Woods boys are no different. After dropping them off at school, I went shopping. It was almost as if Vera hadn't been to the market in six months. They had nothing but the bare minimum. After filling the cabinets and cleaning up, I went to work out and then back to my place to clean. I had been neglecting my own place, so it was nice to tidy up before heading back out to get the boys.

I really don't understand why the previous nannies had issues. The boys are quick, playful, maybe a bit loud—well, the twins are—but I think they're great. When we got home, they rushed to get ready, eating the snack I had ready for them before getting their gear and heading back out the door. The twins had a lot to say about school and even asked for some help with homework, but Charlie didn't talk much. He sat in the front seat, playing on his phone. I tried to get him to talk, but he is pretty tight-lipped. He dragged his ass getting ready, but thankfully, we made it on time.

Especially since Phillip was waiting.

"Charlie is quiet today."

Phillip inhales deeply as he takes a long pull of a soda. "Yeah, it's been like that a lot. He has his outbursts, but there are days when he doesn't talk at all. But then he'll be cool. It's stressing Vera out, which stresses Riana out, and well, you know how that all stresses me out."

I smile. Phillip is a damn good man. "I'm gonna try to talk to him when we get home."

"Good." He then looks over at me. "It seems to get worse when it's almost time to go to his dad's for the weekend. I told Vera I didn't like this setup."

"Yeah. When does she get downtime with them?"

"Exactly. It's dumb."

"Does Charlie not like it there?"

"I think he loves his dad, but he's still angry. The boys tell me that he goes over there and just plays video games, doesn't really talk to anyone. Not even the boys."

"Man, that sucks."

"It does. He'll be okay, though. I'm okay."

I scoff. "After four years of binge drinking and eating."

Phillip pats his flat stomach. He was really overweight when we graduated, but when he met Riana, he went on a diet, and now he thinks he is hot shit. Never does thank me for all the work I put in his ass. "But now, I'm sexy."

I roll my eyes as I lean back, threading my fingers behind my head as I look out to the fields. The twins are on one field while Charlie is on another. It's worked out great. I can sit in the middle and watch both practices. I am finding that though Elliot is quiet, that boy could take out a grown man, and Louis is quick and has a sick wrist shot. Charlie is the whole package, though. He reminds me of myself, knocking dudes out and scoring with ease.

It is fun to watch.

But it reminds me of the Ellenton kids.

Man, I miss them.

Clearing my throat, I ask, "How long do you think she'll keep me on?"

Phillip sits up. "Vera? I'm not sure, but I suspect until Charlie is old enough to drive and is doing it well enough to care for the twins."

So maybe three years.

Three years of not only falling in love with another family but yearning for Vera.

Yeah, that won't be hard at all.

"I'll need to keep my feelings shut down."

Phillip's brows furrow together. "Huh?"

"I don't want to get attached to them and then be left behind."

He slowly nods, though his eyes are on the field. "I hear you. I still think you should get into teaching. Maybe part-time, as an aide or something to get your foot in the door. You could do that now so that when this is over, you teach full-time."

"I thought about doing that, but my sister asked me to help with her baby during the day so she can work. I told her I would."

He shakes his head. "Jenny would understand if you need to get a second job."

"I know, but I want to help with the baby."

"And you're hoping that this gig might go full-time."

I shrug. "Maybe. I mean, it wouldn't be awful if it did. I like the boys."

"They're good kids, but I really don't think, despite how Riana feels, that Vera will pull them. Simon is a piece of work. He wants them at the same school he went to."

"I understand that, but I want to keep my options open."

"Do you, man?" he asks, his eyes wild with annoyance. "Just don't be surprised when I say, 'I told you so.'"

"Oh, you will. First chance you get."

"You know it," he says, sending me a grin, and I laugh. "But really, I can't thank you enough for helping us out with Vera and the boys."

"It's not helping you guys out. I'm getting paid."

"Yeah, but I know how particular you are about families you work for, and they don't meet your standard."

He's right. I usually work with families that have young kids so I can grow with them. Long-term commitment, rather than bouncing from job to job. But this family is different. I knew Charlie and the twins well enough before, and I enjoy them. It doesn't hurt that Vera is really nice to look at. My dating game has taken a back seat to my families the last few years, but something about Vera just makes me want to be close to her. I get the feeling she's strong—stronger than her broken marriage portrays her. And she wants to succeed in parenting as much as she has in her job. I know I can help her with that. It's one of the things I want for them. For me too. She loves her boys. She loves being a mom, and she wants them to be happy. I want to help make them all happy, which is why I took this job. That means I need to ignore the raging hard-on that comes whenever Vera walks into a room.

It's been a really long time since a woman has had me wrung this tightly, and I blame it on the fact that Vera has this air about her that suffocates me but also reminds me that she isn't looking for anything. I don't see a position on Vera's team as a lover. Or anything, for that matter. She is busy with her kids and her job. She has no time for anything else, and I can't blame her.

I'm just her manny.

"True, but the first day is going well."

He scoffs. "Well, let's see if that changes when Simon gets here."

A light bulb goes off with the reminder of Vera's ex. "That's why you're here. You know I can handle a jerk-ass ex."

Phillip laughs as he nods. "I don't doubt that, but I wanted to be here for a buffer. Vera didn't tell him about you yet."

My brow quirks. "Why?"

"Apparently, and don't tell her I told you this, he wants the boys for the spring break she's scheduled to have them and some other shit. Riana told me their call this morning ended with him calling her a bitch and before she could tell him she hired a manny."

Rage fills me within seconds. "Bastard."

Phillip nods. "That he is, so she wouldn't call him back."

"Understandable."

"Yeah," he agrees.

Just as I look up, Charlie is running toward me, pulling off his helmet. I hand him his water bottle.

"Thanks," he says between taking in deep breaths.

"You look great out there," I say, gesturing out at the field. "Keep low, though, when the defense is coming for you."

He nods, downing most of the bottle. "I keep getting cut off when I cut left."

"Then cut right," I say, moving my hands that direction. "Keep them on their toes. You can't always cut left."

"It's my strong side."

"I get that, but if you can go both ways, you'll be an all-around player. Cut right, shoot left, and go bottom right corner if you can."

He slowly nods and then smiles, as if it just dawned on him. "I'll try that."

I smack his thigh. "Attaboy. Go kick some ass."

Charlie grins before handing the bottle back to me, and then he runs off while pulling his helmet back on.

I put the water bottle down, and Phillip eyes me.

"That's the most I've heard him talk in a while."

"Just gotta know how to reach kids. You'll learn it with yours coming."

He scoffs, shaking his head. "Don't remind me, I'm still shaking in my boots."

"You'll be great."

"Maybe I can just hire you to teach me your ways."

"Ha. You can't afford me," I tease.

As his laughter dies off, my attention turns to the twins. They are running up the field, and I laugh when I see they're on the same line together. "Oh, they messed up putting those two together."

Phillip laughs. "Oh, yeah. I wonder why they're just now doing that?"

"I'm not sure, but I like it!"

Phillip nods as he scoots to the edge of his seat, and I do the same, resting my elbows on my knees as the boys rush up the field. Elliot is in front, smacking people left and right, while Louis follows behind him, holding the ball in his net as he moves around the bodies that Elliot lays out. Louis cuts to the right of Elliot as if he is going to pass, but I know the kid wouldn't. Not with his shot.

And when the ball hits the back of the goal, I stand up, pumping my fist hard. "Thataway, Woods!"

Phillip stands beside me, cheering just as loudly. When the boys look back at us, I throw my hands up, waving them obnoxiously, which makes them both grin as they run back up the field.

I smack Phillip playfully. "Great play."

"Lethal together."

I go to agree, but before I can, someone says, "I've been saying to put them together for years."

I don't recognize the voice. When I look to Phillip, he's nodding. "Yeah, you have. How are you, Simon?" He holds his hand out as I try to lift my jaw off the ground.

This is Simon?

What in the fuck?

I know I'm tall, but this dude is short. Like maybe five foot seven, and he is pudgy. He has a belly, and he looks old. His eyes are light but beady-looking, and he's got one hell of a receding hairline. I know that I probably don't like this guy for what he has done to Vera, but come on, he left her?

Vera is easily a ten. This dude is maybe a four.

Moving my gaze from his, I take in who I assume is the ex-nanny. She's pretty, I guess, but she isn't Vera. She looks like the kind of girl who is stuck in high school, looking for the next guy to take care of her. Vera is a woman; she doesn't need anyone to take care of her. Being wanted by Vera would be like winning the lottery.

A hundred times over.

Phillip jerks his head to me. "Lincoln, this is the boys' father, Simon."

I hold out my hand. "Hey, nice to meet you."

"You too," he says, shaking my hand quickly before looking back out at the field. "Okay, we're gonna go over on the other side, say hi, and then head out. We have reservations in the city."

Phillip says, "Sounds good."

Without another word, he takes his lady's hand, and they walk away together. I notice people watching, I assume saying the same things I'm thinking. He left Vera for that chick? What a dumbass.

"Is he insane?" I ask.

"Huh?" Phillip mutters. He's on his phone, probably texting Riana.

I sit down. "He left Vera for that?"

Phillip shakes his head. "Yeah, I don't get it. Except from what I heard, he didn't like how big Vera got. She used to be super skinny when they were younger, but after she had the twins, she had a hard time losing the weight."

"There is no weight to lose," I say.

He looks up from his phone, and his brow rises. "No?"

"No, she's perfect the way she is. He's a fucking idiot."

Phillip sings, "Someone has a crush."

I scoff and look away. "A crush, please. I know a gorgeous woman when I see one, and Vera is all that. Her ass is mind-blowing, and that waist, Jesus. She's gorgeous, and that girl is nothing compared to her." When I'm met with silence, I look over to see Phillip watching me with narrowed eyes. "What?" I ask.

He shakes his head. "You know she's off-limits."

I'm a little taken aback by that. I mean, I know that, but I don't want to believe it. And I sure as hell don't want my buddy telling me that. "Well, duh," I say. "She's my boss."

"Exactly. She needs you to help, and there can be no distractions. *None.* She needs to work and care for the boys. She doesn't need you playing with her feelings."

I laugh out loud at that. "Play with her feelings? Do you even know me?"

"I know that you haven't settled down the whole time I've known you. You're a fuck 'em and leave 'em type."

I balk at that. "What the hell, Phillip! I am not! I just haven't found anyone to settle down with!"

He eyes me. "In what, almost twenty years?" he exaggerates.

I shrug. "Maybe so! I don't know. I dated Amelia for a long time."

"And she left you because she wanted to wait to have kids."

"Exactly, but I was committed as hell to her and loved her deeply. She broke up with me, played with my feelings, not the other way around."

He shrugs. "Whatever. Vera isn't the one."

"Never said she was," I say. "I can't believe you think that."

"I didn't mean to offend you, but seriously, I don't even remember your last girlfriend, besides Amelia, and let's be honest, you don't go long without sex."

"Just 'cause I'm not like you and Riana doesn't mean I'm having sex with everyone."

His brows come together once more. "So, you haven't been banging your neighbor?"

I laugh. "Melissa? She moved like two years ago."

He looks away, thinking that over. "Oh, she did?"

"Yeah," I say, shaking my head. "I'm not what you think I am."

He doesn't answer, and I'm okay with that. I'm pissed he thought that of me. I'm a lot of things, but I don't go out wanting to hurt anyone like he implied. Plus, I'd never hurt Vera. I'd make sweet and dirty love to her beautiful body, and I'd care for her as much as she'd allow me to. I know darn well she doesn't have time for anything more than that, and I'm okay with that. I don't even know her. How could I want more?

"Just promise me. Leave her alone," Phillip says suddenly.

I look over at him, surprised by his request. "Really?"

"Yeah, dude. She worries me. Things have been rough,

and Riana stresses so much. I don't want you getting involved and shit going down funky, and then I lose my best friend. Just do your job. Do what you said; keep your feelings in check."

I swallow hard and slowly nod. He's right, and let's be honest, nothing would ever happen. I know that, but it sucks to think that if it did, I wouldn't be able to do anything about it.

"Yeah, man. No problem."

And with that, I sealed my fate.

And boy, does it feel all kinds of wrong.

# CHAPTER SIX

## VERA

The ride in from the city is always very relaxing for me.

But not today.

I left early with a box full of work I plan on finishing over the weekend. With Kaia coming alone to get the boys, I want to be there. I also haven't told Simon about Lincoln yet, so I need to be there just in case. I don't want Kaia getting information out of Lincoln. Ugh, I don't want to face her, and I sure as hell don't want to talk to her. While I'm trying my best to accept that my husband is gone, I don't think I'll ever accept that he was taken by someone I considered my best friend. And Kaia was that. My number two after Riana.

Not that I'd ever tell Riana that.

When my phone rings, I dig for it. I shouldn't be surprised it's Riana.

"Hey," I say.

"Hey, what time will you be home?"

I check the map on the train and compare the station we've just passed to the current stop. "In about twenty minutes."

"Huh? I thought today was your late night?"

"It is, but Kaia is coming to get the boys since Simon is out of town for the night, so I want to be there. I still haven't told him about Lincoln."

"Vera," she chastises, and I roll my eyes.

"I know. I just haven't gotten around to it."

And I also don't want to talk to him. While I know he'll have a lot to say about a man caring for my children, I have to admit, my earlier reservations about it are gone. Lincoln is amazing. Yes, it's only been three days, but the house is cleaner than it's ever been, there is food in the fridge, and my kids are happy. Well, the twins are happy, and Charlie has only grunted at me twice. We didn't even get into it last night, which is usually how every Thursday has gone since his mood plummets by the end of the week. He dreads going to his dad's, so the drama the last day or two of the week is predictable now. But this week was a little better, and I have to think it had something to do with our manny.

"You need to tell him. It's only making it worse, waiting."

"I know." I groan, closing my eyes as I lean my head on the window. The rumble of the train makes the contents of my box shift a bit. "I'll tell him Sunday."

"Good."

"Or maybe Saturday at the boys' games."

"Even better. I think we're gonna go."

"Oh nice," I say with a smile, but it falls when I consider telling her about my date with Dennis.

Before I can, she asks, "Are you working all weekend?"

I clear my throat. "Yeah, which reminds me, I think I'm gonna talk to Richard about working weekends instead of late during the week so I can be home to spend more time with the boys before they go to Simon's."

"Yeah, that's a good plan."

"I think so," I say slowly, and then I clear my throat. "I have a date Saturday."

She squeaks. "Really! With who?"

"The guy from accounting. Dennis."

"Ooooo! Is he hot?"

I shrug. "He's okay."

"But he isn't Lincoln."

"Riana! Please."

As if I need the reminder of Lincoln's hotness. I don't, especially when all my wet dreams circle around him and the way his back flexes when he is replacing light bulbs in my kitchen. Even through his shirt, I could see every single muscle. I wanted to beg him to screw in light bulbs everywhere and then screw me.

Pathetic, I know.

"I'm still pulling for Lincoln."

I scoff. "Pulling? For what? You're insane!"

"I don't know... The more I think about it, the more I like it. He would complement you."

I'm dumbfounded. "Huh? Did you hit your head today?"

She giggles. "Nope, right mind, and I think it would do you both good."

"Do us both good?" I pause before lowering my voice. "Riana, we don't even know each other. At this point, I don't need any complications. Getting involved with Lincoln would be complicated. I just need sex with a willing man."

She scoffs. "Well, bet ya ten bucks you won't do Dennis

and think of Dennis. Your mind will be consumed by Lincoln. Do you know he has abs? Like thick ones. He's the one who got Phillip in shape."

Information I did not need to know.

"I am disgusted by you," I say, pressing my hand to my chest. "This man is the caregiver of my children. He's not just some piece of ass."

She's too busy laughing. "Whatever. You watch. I'll get to tell you, 'I told you so' in no time."

"You will not," I say just as the train slows at my stop. "I'll call you back."

"Drive safe!" she yells, but I don't answer.

I know I'll hear about this later. I don't need to think of Lincoln like that. Harmless fantasies are one thing, but giving myself false hope is another. Riana is encouraging my lust for the manny! Which blows my mind! Doesn't she realize that if I did jump in the sheets, the boys would suffer?

If I learned anything from my divorce, it's don't sleep with the nanny.

Or manny.

Whatever.

Throwing everything in my car, I check and realize I have plenty of time to get home. After a short drive, I pull into the driveway beside Lincoln's SUV. When I reach the door, arms full of work, he is waiting for me.

His hair is tousled, like he has been running his fingers through it over and over again. The shirt he wears is loose-fitting but tight on his shoulders. His biceps are bulging, and when the hell did I start to think forearms are sexy?

Breathless, I give him a smile as he reaches for the box.

"I didn't know you were coming home early," he says.

"Yeah, their father's wife is coming to get them. I wanted to be here for that."

I point to the table. "You can put that there."

"Cool," he says.

I try so hard not to watch the way his back moves, but apparently, along with beards, I'm becoming attracted to backs.

*Get it together, Woods.*

Clearing my throat, I say, "You can go home."

"Oh," he says, and then he points to the kitchen. "I was in the middle of cleaning out the fridge. I thought I had more time before you got home."

Unsure what to say, I stumble on my words. "Oh, that's okay, I can finish it."

He points to the box, and with each motion he takes, a new whiff of his cologne almost knocks me on my ass. "Looks like you have a lot more to do than what I started."

*Get your head right, Woods!*

Though he is right, I don't want to admit it. When I meet his gaze, he is smiling, and I'm not sure how, but I smile back at him. "Okay—"

But before I can finish, the doorbell rings.

"Son of a bitch," I mutter. I feel Lincoln move behind me to look through the peephole.

"Ah, the wife."

I groan. "The wife," I say before I reach for the door. "Boys, let's go." After I open the door, I move out of the way.

"They're going to be a second. I just walked in. I thought you wouldn't be here until six." Without waiting for her to answer, I head to the bottom of the stairs. "Boys," I holler once more. I hear them moving.

"I was over on this side of town, and Simon told me to come get them."

I don't look at her. "Can you call next time?"

"Yeah, I guess I should have," Kaia says, her voice very unsure.

My heart is heavy as I watch the boys run back and forth upstairs, gathering their things. I had hoped to have dinner with them before they left. This is beyond annoying, but this is my new normal. I have to remember that.

"You were at practice."

I look back at the sound of Kaia's voice to find her talking to Lincoln. She looks small beside him. Before, she was always so put together, hair always done and nails perfectly manicured, but that isn't how she looks today. Her hair is a mess, and while she's still dressed to the nines, I don't miss the paleness in her face or that her nails are chewed to the quick. I shouldn't find joy in this, but in some sick way I do, because the woman who stole my husband looks like shit.

"Phillip's friend," she says, as a statement rather than a question.

Lincoln nods. "Yup, that's me. Lincoln Scott."

They shake hands before she looks back at me and then grins. It's the way she used to grin at me when we found a guy good-looking on one of the many girl dates we had. We were so close, but she ruined that. Just as quick as the grin came, it is gone when I set her with a look. She looks away, threading her fingers over her growing stomach.

Ugh, I'm so pissed.

"Nice to meet you," she purrs.

I don't usually want to throat punch people, but Kaia is high up there on my list.

Lincoln doesn't answer as the twins come running down the stairs. They're dressed and ready to go, which is a surprise. Another sign of how Lincoln has changed things. I thought they'd take longer. Coming toward me, they drop their bags before they wrap themselves around me.

Elliot squeezes me. "I thought we'd get to see you before we go."

"I'm sorry, love. Kaia was on this side of town and wanted to get you guys early," I say, kissing their heads. "Don't worry, I'll be at the game tomorrow. And then Sunday, we'll watch movies and eat loads of crap food that Lincoln bought."

Elliot smiles up at me. "Sounds like fun."

I beam down at their beautiful faces. Though their looks favor Simon, that would never change how much I love them. They are my little balls of sunshine. "What do you think, Louis?" I ask.

Finally looking up at me, he shrugs. "I don't want to go."

"I know, my love, but you have to."

"And we're gonna have so much fun! We're going to the movies tonight," Kaia says. But neither boy looks at her.

"Why? Isn't Dad gone?" Charlie's voice comes from the top of the stairs.

I look up at him as the twins' hands thread with mine.

Three little squeezes taking my breath away.

"Yes, but I thought we could go together," Kaia says then, but Charlie doesn't seem interested. He comes down the stairs, facing me.

"I thought we were eating dinner first," Charlie groans.

"She came early 'cause she was on this side of town, no need to drive all over," I tell him as the boys move. Reaching for my oldest, I pull him in close. "Please be good. Don't be mouthy?"

He scoffs at my neck. "I don't want to go to the movies with her."

"I understand, but she is your stepmom," I say, pulling back and cupping his face in my hands. "Be respectful."

His brown eyes mirror mine as he slowly nods. "I'll try."

Well, I can't ask for more. He is having such a hard time, and yesterday's therapy session hadn't gone well.

"Thank you," I say, kissing his cheek. He attempts to move away, but I get him anyway. Sending him a grin, I take his hand in mine and squeeze it three times. His eyes widen, but by the grace of God, a small smile fills his face. "I'll see you tomorrow at the game. Call me if you need me."

"I will," he says, moving past me, and when I turn, I see the boys are waiting for him. With his shoulders back, he walks with them toward Kaia. Clearing his throat, he says, "I don't want to go to the movies. Do you guys?"

Like I knew they would, the boys agree with him as they walk out the door, leaving Kaia behind. She looks back at me, dejection in her eyes, but I just stare at her with the fiery depths of hell swirling in mine.

"Guess I'll go," she says.

"Guess you will," I say with my chin high, and without another word, she leaves my house, shutting the door behind her.

"Shit. I wouldn't want to be on the other side of that ice-cold gaze."

I look at Lincoln. I had forgotten he was there. "Oh. Yeah. She isn't my favorite person."

"No?" he asks with a laugh. "I thought she was your bestie."

"Used to be," I say, heading to the kitchen. "Not anymore. For obvious reasons."

"No shit," he says, following behind me. "I thought she was just the nanny."

I exhale hard, not wanting to rehash this. "She worked for us for a while. We became close."

"That sucks," he says, and he sounds genuinely upset for me. As if he gets how awful it was for me to find out my best friend stole my husband. It's nice and doesn't help me at all with keeping my feelings at bay for him. His voice is so damn deep and throaty. Raspy almost. All I can do is picture him whispering the dirtiest things in my ear with that voice.

I shake my head to get those thoughts out of my head before I say, "It is what it is."

Ignoring the mess around me, I go into the cabinet and reach to the very back for a bottle of wine. Pouring a hearty glass, I lean into the counter and then take a long sip. The sip doesn't take away the pain of watching my boys go with Kaia, but it at least gives me the promise of not giving a fuck by the time I'm done with the glass. If that doesn't work, I have at least three more bottles hidden in the kitchen.

"You hide your wine?"

I open my eyes to find Lincoln watching me, his eyes dark as he grips the counter. Swallowing, I nod. "I had to when Riana was staying here all the time. She doesn't like when I drink."

"Really? I didn't know she had an issue with it," he says, leaning his hip into the island as he looks at me. He is so large, so thick, and Jesus, beautiful.

"You know we lost our parents, right?" When he nods, I go on. "It was by a drunk driver."

He presses his lips together. "I'm sorry."

"Thank you, but because of that, she doesn't want me drinking. She does the same thing to Phillip too."

"She doesn't do it to me."

I smile. "You don't have kids who would be left behind," I answer.

He nods. "Yeah, I guess I don't." There is a certain sadness in his eyes that follows that statement.

I take another long sip of my wine. While he works on the mess that is my fridge, I watch him for a moment. I could take my glass upstairs and soak in the bath, where I'd probably cry for hours, or I could get to know the guy who is caring for my sons. While I'm always ready for a nice cry fest, I really want to know Lincoln.

"So your family lives here?"

He nods as he wipes down the bottom shelf of the fridge. "Yup, on the other side of town. My dad is a truck driver, and my mom is a stay-at-home grandma since all her kids have moved out. My second oldest sister comes in and out a lot. She can't seem to get her shit together."

I lean my glass against my cheek. "Happens."

"It does," he says, glancing over at me. "She's a good sister. Not my favorite but good."

I laugh. "How many do you have?"

"Six."

"Good Lord!"

He laughs. "Yeah, I'm the baby. I'll let your imagination run wild on how that was."

*Don't you dare do that, Woods.*

If I did, my heart might not be able to handle it. Clearing my throat, I ask, "So that's why you like kids?"

"Yeah, I guess. I grew up with no say whatsoever with seven women, but once my sisters started having kids, I was always the one to take care of them. I don't know. I just like kids."

"That's cute," I say, and I mean it.

"Are you making fun of me, Ms. Woods?"

Oh, the way he says my name is dangerous. Breathless, I attempt a smile. "No sir, I am not. I may have found it weird at the beginning, but maybe I was just being a judgmental bitch."

His lips quirk as I take another long gulp of my wine. "You found it weird?"

"Yeah, Riana told me about you before the long line of nannies who didn't work out, but I didn't want to go with you because you were male. A male nanny was weird to me, but now, I think you're better at being a mom than I am."

His brows pull together. "That's not true. I could never be

you. Your boys adore you. Honestly. They talk about you all the time."

My heart warms. "They do?"

"They do. Charlie isn't as vocal, but he loves you."

I want to cry. Turning around, I reach for the bottle and take another sip. "He makes me nervous."

"I bet."

"He isn't handling all this well, and the therapist isn't happy with his progress. I just don't want him to end up like Phillip did. Drinking his way through college and letting himself go." When I'm met with his hearty laughter, I smile. "What? It's true!"

"I know. I was right there with him through those times. We had some fun."

Oh, I know they did, though I don't say that. "I don't want that for Charlie."

Lincoln nods in agreement. "I don't think Charlie will end up like that. Especially with having Phillip as an uncle. He can learn from Phillip's mistakes."

"Yeah." I let out a long sigh. "I hope you're right."

"I wouldn't worry too much. Phillip had some inner demons that no one could understand. Charlie is well-rounded. He's just upset his family isn't what society deems as normal. He's finding his bearings. He's a great kid."

My heart soars. "Thank you. I think so too."

Swirling my glass, I glance over at him, and our gazes meet. His eyes go dark, and heat rushes through my body. It gathers between my legs as I watch his lips part slightly. He slowly wipes a small plastic container of butter, and all I can think is that I wish he'd open it and rub it on me.

What in the world?

Shaking my head, I pull my gaze from his. "So are you married?"

He scoffs. "No."

"Girlfriend?"

"Nope."

"Boyfriend?"

His head jerks up, and then he laughs. "Why does everyone assume I'm gay!"

"That's a no, right?"

"No, I'm not," he says with a dry look.

I grin at him, and I'm two seconds from snorting with laughter.

"You knew that, though."

"I did. Riana told me. I just wanted to make sure."

He rolls his eyes. "Well, I'm not."

"Good," I say, and honestly, I don't know why I said that. I don't care if he is dating.

Right?

"Good?" he asks, his eyes teasing mine.

I blink. "I don't know why I said that."

"You don't?" A slow grin pulls at his lips, almost like he is fighting back his laughter.

"I don't," I say quickly, and then I take a pull of my wine, his laughter filling the room. "Sorry. I shouldn't have pried like that."

"Why not?" He's watching me, his eyes hungry and his lips wet as if he just licked them.

I want to take a picture so that I can show Riana how he looks at me! Like he wants to eat me. The thing is, I'd let him in a heartbeat.

"Because it's none of my business," I say simply.

He shrugs. "It can be."

My eyes widen.

He continues to grin, his eyes full of lust. "Are you seeing anyone?"

I scrunch up my face in confusion. Why does he care? "Why?"

"Just asking. Getting to know you."

"Shouldn't you ask what my favorite color is before you ask if I'm dating?"

He holds my gaze. "You asked me."

He had me there. "Oh, well. I guess I do have a date tomorrow."

He scoffs. "You guess?"

I shrug, shaking my head. "Riana pushed me into finding someone to have sex with. So I chose the guy from accounting." I pause. "Why in the hell am I telling you that?"

His laughter fills the room, and it's such a deep sound, something I hadn't heard before. "You feel comfortable," he decides, his eyes moving along my face, and once more, I'm breathless. Am I comfortable? How'd that happen? "So you chose a guy from accounting?"

I find myself giggling as I shake my head. "He isn't my type, but I need something. Or better yet, Riana says I need something. I don't know. It's stupid."

He doesn't say anything, moving the rag along the shelf

for the milk and tea before putting them back in the fridge. "Shouldn't you choose someone you want, though?"

My heart jumps up into my throat as our gazes lock once more. I don't know what it is about the pull his eyes have, but man, they capture me. "I don't exactly have a line of men wanting to take me out."

"Maybe you just don't see them."

I can only blink, unsure what he means by that. I think I know, but is that just my vagina being hopeful? "I'll probably cancel."

"I think you should."

"You do?"

"Yeah, you're obviously not into him."

"True, but apparently I'm not supposed to be into him. I just need to have sex." His lips quirk, and I smile back. "From what Riana says... And wow, this wine is making me loosey goosey."

That makes him laugh. "My mom says that after a bottle."

I hold my glass to him. "Smart woman."

"She is," he says as he puts the rest of the stuff back in the fridge. He throws the rag in the sink and then washes his hands. He's right there. All I have to do is reach out and touch him. Take what I want, but I won't.

I need him.

Looking over his shoulder at me, he says, "She'd always say don't waste a good fuck on someone who doesn't matter."

I blink. "Your mom says fuck?"

His face lights up. "She does."

"She sounds like my kind of person."

"She'd probably say the same about you," he says, leaning against the sink as he dries his hands. "She'd also commend you on how you acted with the boys toward that chick. You don't owe it to her to be nice."

I look away, running my fingers along the bottom of my glass as I lean back into the counter by the sink. "I refuse to give them the opportunity to speak badly about me to them. If I'm nice to them, the boys won't believe them even if they say terrible things."

Leaning into me, he says, "They wouldn't believe it anyway. You're their mom."

His gaze takes mine once more, and I swear, all I have to do is move an inch, and my lips would crash against his. I turn my view to his lips and swallow hard, but he moves away, grinning. "I guess I'm done."

"Oh, yeah, you are."

Our eyes meet once more, and I know I couldn't look away if I wanted. I feel the heat coming off his beautiful body, and I want so badly to touch him. But what if I'm reading him all wrong? What if he doesn't want me, but pities me? I couldn't take that rejection at all.

Licking his lips, he says, "So, I guess if you don't need me for anything else, I'll head out."

*Well, if you're offering sex, then I may...*

I don't say that, though. I just shake my head. "Nope, I have a date with my bathtub and then some work to do."

He slowly nods. "Sounds like a blast."

"Oh, yeah. I party hard on Fridays."

We share a grin as he moves past me, his spicy, cedar,

and tobacco scent tickling my senses. When he reaches the entryway, he looks back at me, and a very suggestive grin pulls at his lips. "I'm just a call away."

And then he's gone.

Leaving me speechless, and I swear no one has ever done that to me.

Maybe it was his tone that left me speechless, because what I heard is, "Call me if you wanna fuck."

I need help.

I need Jesus.

Fuck, I need to get laid.

# CHAPTER SEVEN

### VERA

When Phillip taps my knee, I grin over at him. "I appreciate you coming with me to do that. I hate trying to surprise Riana. It's so hard," he says.

I nod as I send an email back to my boss with an update on all the work I did the night before. I send him a grin. "Of course. You know I love shopping."

"You also know how hard it is to surprise her," Phillip reminds me.

"That too," I agree before laughing softly.

His laughter fills the car. Riana wasn't the only lucky one when she picked Phillip way back when. I remember thinking that I'd never like him. He was too cocky and full of himself, but he proved me wrong. He is by far the nicest man I have ever met, and he cares for me, which is refreshing. He's a good guy, and I love him dearly, so when he asked me to help him with ideas about a nursery for Riana, I didn't hesitate to agree. I wanted to go, and I am honored he asked me.

"Yup," he says as he turns out of the city.

We are heading back to pick up Riana before the boys' games. I am dreading seeing Simon and Kaia, but I am thankful that Riana and Phillip will be there. Maybe then I won't have to talk to either of them.

"So how's Lincoln working out?"

Ugh. Just his name has me squirming in my seat.

Before I went to bed last night, I thought of him. One thing led to another, and I got myself off so damn good that I am still riding the high. I haven't done that in what feels like forever, and all it did was make me desperate for the real thing. I sort of regretted canceling my date with Dennis, but I just kept hearing Lincoln's husky words over and over in my head.

*Don't waste a good fuck on someone who doesn't matter.*

I know darn well his momma didn't say that, which means he was saying that to me, and something about that gave me gooseflesh all over my body.

But also confused me all to hell.

Unable to tell my brother-in-law of the complete and utter knots that man has me in, I smile. "He's been great. The boys adore him."

"I knew they would. He's a great guy."

"He seems like it," I say offhandedly. "I haven't gotten to know him very well yet."

He scoffs. "That's surprising. He talks all the time."

I quirk my brow at that. "Hm. He doesn't around me. But we haven't had a lot of time. I'm usually blazing through as he's going out."

"Really?"

"I mean, we chit-chatted a bit last night, but nothing like getting to know him."

He slowly nods as he moves in his chair. "Maybe we can

all go out tonight."

That excites me way more than it should, but before I can agree to it, my phone is ringing. It's Charlie. "Hey, love, what's up?'

"Mom, I left my crosse in Lincoln's car."

"Oh, crap," I say, and I notice that Phillip looks toward me. "Charlie left his lacrosse gear in Lincoln's car."

"Okay, I'll call him," Phillip says. "We can swing by and grab it on the way to the house."

"Your uncle is the best. He's in the car with me, and we will swing through and grab it before meeting you at the field."

"Cool. Thanks, Mom."

"Of course, love."

"Okay, see you in a bit. Love you," he says, and then the line goes dead before I can scream I love him back. It's been months since he has said that. I don't doubt that he loves me. But hearing the words... Oh, they fill me with such joy. My face breaks into a grin as Phillip calls Lincoln. Man, I don't think Charlie realizes that made my day.

As we wait for Lincoln's voice to come across the car speakers through Bluetooth, I pray Phillip doesn't notice how eager I am to hear Lincoln's voice. I want to ask to go in with him to get the crosse, but I worry he'll think I have a thing for his best friend. Well, not a *thing*. That's silly. I just lust for him. Yes, that sounds more appropriate. More scandalous, but eh, no one will ever know.

But man, what a hell of a scandal it would be...

Unfortunately, Lincoln doesn't answer.

"What the hell? I know he's home," Phillip says.

"How do you know that?"

"He told me he isn't doing anything today. He's probably on the phone with his mom. He'll call back."

It's funny how close they are. They are almost like Riana and me. Lincoln doesn't call back, so Phillip heads to his condo, which is on the other side of Riana and Phillip's complex. I wring my fingers together as we pull into the driveway. Nervously, I ask, "You don't think you should call again?"

He shakes his head, throwing the car door open. "He's home, and I have a key. Come on."

Quickly, I say, "Oh, I'll wait here."

"Just come on. We'll probably start talking, and I'll feel bad leaving you out here."

I want to see Lincoln's home. I'm sure it's annoyingly clean.

Cleanest man I've ever met.

Yup, my curiosity gets the best out of me, and I follow him up the walkway as Phillip digs out his keys and opens the door with ease. "Bro."

"What?" Lincoln calls through the house as we enter his entryway. Of course, it's cleaner than a hospital room. I have shoes and the boys' things everywhere.

"Hey, asshole, I've been calling you," Phillip yells and then groans. "Jesus, put some clothes on."

I should be embarrassed with how I stretch my neck around my brother-in-law to see. When my gaze falls on Lincoln in only a very small yellow ducky towel, I'm nothing but thankful as my mouth parts in awe. Riana wasn't lying; he is ripped from the top of his shoulders to his thighs. Each bit of him defined and thick with muscle. The ducky towel doesn't

TONI ALEO

cover much, and I swear I can see the length of him through it.

And that alone has me gasping for air.

He must have not seen me, because a slow and very naughty grin comes across his sexy face. "Hey, Vera. Didn't see you there."

I can't talk.

"Yeah, can you go get dressed?"

*No. Please don't.*

Not that I can say that as my eyes take in every single inch of Lincoln. He is either sweaty or he just got out of the shower, because drops run down his chest, getting lost in the fabric that he is struggling to hold at his waist. "Fuck off. I was working out."

*Oh. Oh, God.*

"In a dish towel?"

He scoffs. "No, I was working out, and I heard you come in so I grabbed this."

"You still work out naked. Ew," Phillip teases, and Lincoln just laughs.

Naked. He works out naked.

*Jesus, Mary, and Joseph.*

It is beyond unfair that sight isn't televised.

When a sound leaves my lips, almost a moan, I turn bright red. Well that is until I notice Phillip looking at me funny, so of course, I cover it with a cough.

"Need some water, Vera?"

My eyes cut to Lincoln's, and I swear he is teasing me! He runs his tongue along his lips, and I squeeze my thighs together and ogle him.

What is he doing to me?

"Whatever. Charlie left his crosse in your car. Came to pick it up before we head to the game."

Lincoln points to the couch, but I don't move. I'm too busy gawking at him like a girl in the front row at a Justin Timberlake concert, praying for him to sweat on me. Newsflash: if Lincoln starts gyrating, I might pass out.

Meanwhile, no one notices that I am two seconds from passing out as Lincoln says, "I was going to bring it with me."

"You're coming?" I squeak, and Phillip gives me a look once more, which leads to more really bad coughing. "Something is in my throat."

"I have that glass for you if you need it," Lincoln says, his voice so low and dangerous, but I shake my head quickly as he looks back to Phillip. "I was about to jump in the shower before you walked in."

"Oh, okay. We'll just grab it now so he has it," Phillip says as he looks back at me for confirmation.

I nod. "Yup."

Lincoln pulls his brows together. "You okay?"

"Great," I say, my heart jackhammering in my chest. I'm trying so hard not to look at his chiseled chest and rock-hard abs, but it's a damn fail. My eyes cut back to Lincoln, and he's watching me, his eyes full of playfulness as his lips curve. I don't know how I am ever going to look at this man and not think of this moment for the rest of my existence, but I am thankful for it.

I am going to get myself off good tonight.

"What are you doing afterwards?" Phillip asks.

I hadn't even noticed that Phillip had moved and grabbed the crosse.

Tearing his gaze from mine, Lincoln inhales hard before shrugging. "Same thing I always do... Hang out, watch TV, and sleep."

"Loser," Phillip teases.

Lincoln scoffs. "Hey, before you were waiting on Riana, hand and foot, you were doing the same."

"I was," he says fondly, and then he shakes his head. "I think we're going to dinner. Wanna join us?"

"Who's us?" Lincoln asks, his eyes moving between the two of us.

Phillip gives him a dry look. "What does that mean? It's me, Riana, and Vera. Why are you being weird?"

"I'm not," he says simply, his eyes snapping back to mine. He loses a bit of the dish towel, which gives me one hell of a peek at the crook of his leg. I'm pretty sure my tongue is hanging out of my mouth at this point. "Is that cool with you, boss lady?"

"Huh?"

He smiles widely, his face so bright, and those teeth— fucking hell, he's beautiful. It's unfair. "Is it okay if I come to dinner with you guys?'

"Oh, oh, yes, of course. I told Phillip in the car, I wanted to get to know you."

"You do, do you?" he asks, and once more heat flushes through my body. "I'd like that."

I can only blink as Phillip's phone goes off. "It's Riana. She's ready."

"Oh! Well, let's go!" I say, turning quickly and almost running into the couch.

"Easy there."

I look back to Lincoln and see his gaze moving along my body, and he smiles. "It's nice seeing you in jeans for a change."

Another weird noise leaves my lips, and Lincoln sends me a grin that is probably how a wolf looks in a chicken coop.

I'm the poor little chicken.

My brother-in-law must be oblivious to it all. He reaches for the door and looks back at Lincoln. "Your towel is about to snap. You better get a new one."

Lincoln laughs. "Eh, it's 'cause my cock's too big."

I run into the doorframe.

Right smack dab into it.

Good God Almighty, kill me now.

"Shit. You okay, Vera?"

"Fine," I somehow get out, holding my forehead.

"Asshole. Watch it around my sister-in-law."

Lincoln looks at me and laughs almost in a teasing way. "She's a grown woman. She knows what a cock is."

Oh boy, do I. And at this moment, with my head throbbing and my pussy dripping wet, all I want is his.

In my mouth.

# CHAPTER EIGHT

## VERA

"I shit you not."

Riana's eyes widen. "No!"

"Yes," I whisper, my eyes wide. "The towel was like one of those little dish ones that you hang by the sink. He had somehow wrapped that around him, and I swear to God, Riana, I'll never look at rubber duckies the same."

She snorts with laughter. "Rubber duckies?"

I shrug. "No clue, but they were straining across his hips and thighs. Jesus, those thighs."

"And it was all there."

"All of it," I gasp, my eyes falling shut, seeing it as if it is in front of me at that moment. "He is so thick."

Her eyes glitter with excitement. "What did you do?"

"What else could I do? Phillip was right there! I was just trying to breathe and not attack him!"

She giggles as she leans into me, which means we are basically sharing my lawn chair. She has a way of doing that, getting in my space—not that I mind. Too much. "I am so jealous he has a great body...though, Phillip's is better."

"You have to say that," I say dryly, and she nods. "And I

love you, and Phillip, but Lincoln's is way better."

"Ugh," she adds and then her eyes go to where Phillip, Charlie, and Lincoln are standing by the side of the field, cheering the twins on. "I wonder what he was thinking as you gawked at him."

"I swear he loved it."

"No!"

"Yes! And he was teasing me, licking his lips and giving me those 'come tear this towel off me, baby, with your teeth' eyes."

Her laughter is so loud as she falls back in her chair, shaking her head. When I say *loud*, I mean everyone turns to look at her. Even Phillip and Lincoln, who both give her a weird look before looking back at the field. Charlie pays her no mind; he is used to his crazy aunt Riana. "You are insane. Legit, stop it."

My eyes widen. "No, really," I insist. "You don't understand. He seriously looks at me like that."

"That is crazy talk. He's so nice."

"And either, a: a closet freak, or b: knows I want him and is dead-set on driving me out of my skin."

"If he knew, he'd come after you."

I scoff. "He would not!"

"Yes, he would. I just know it."

"You're insane." I'm answered with her giggles, which has me grinning as I shake my head. "It's totally unfair, and the only good thing is I'll get off so much faster tonight."

Again, she almost falls out of the chair. "Who's the freak, Vera Woods?"

I giggle as the men look back at us, both shaking their

heads, but I don't care. Exhaling hard, I drink in his back and then his thick legs. "Ugh, Ri, I can't handle it. I really can't."

"Well too bad. You got to."

"Well, duh," I say simply, reality hitting me in the face. "The boys adore him."

Her laughter has subsided by now as she throws her legs into my lap, her gaze toward where Phillip stands with Lincoln and Charlie. "They really do. Charlie seems better, or am I just hopeful?"

"Well, he hasn't pranked anyone in five days, and he hasn't screamed at me either. He actually told me he loved me today."

Her eyes light up. "He did?"

"Yeah, on the phone. I don't think he meant to, but he did."

"Oh, V."

She takes my hand, squeezing it hard, and I smile widely at her. "I'm not naïve enough to think that he's great and things are all good. I know he still has some healing to do, but I truly think we are heading in the right direction."

She beams at me. "Told ya."

"Told ya, what?" I ask, taking a long pull of my water.

"Lincoln would be great for you guys."

I scoff. "I mean, I don't doubt his magic or whatever he does with the boys to make sure they are clean at all hours of the day, but I highly doubt his being around Charlie for three days changed him."

"No, but it is giving him a male presence, someone he can talk to."

I look away. I want him to talk to me. "Have you heard that they've been talking?"

"I asked Phillip, but he said that Lincoln hasn't said anything."

"Oh, okay," I say sadly. "I need Lincoln to take Charlie to therapy on Thursday. I need to work a bit late."

"He won't mind."

"I know, but I like being there."

"I understand that, but at least someone he trusts will be."

"Does he trust him?" I ask, my gaze falling on them. Lincoln said something funny, and my baby is grinning so wide, his laughter is making my smile. "They don't even know him."

"But they do. Lincoln hangs with us a lot."

"How did I never meet him?"

Riana pauses and then shrugs. "You were always working." I move my fingers through my hair, and Riana adds, "You've cut down on your hours so much, Vera. Please don't be upset."

"I'm fine," I lie, and I know she doesn't believe me. "I just wish I could have met him before he became my *manny*."

Riana cuts a look to me. "You were married."

I twist my lips in dissatisfaction. "Wow. Guess I'll never get my chance with him."

Riana grins. "Why not?"

"If he's as good as you're saying, I can't risk ruining it for some hot sex," I whisper as I watch him wrap his arm around Charlie, squeezing him as they laugh.

"Ah, I disagree."

"What? How?"

"Hey, I understand what you're saying, but jeez, Vera, you haven't had a good time with someone since before Simon cheated on you the first time. You're due."

I consider that, but while I agree, I know that it is all a long shot. "None of this matters."

She makes a face. "Why?"

"Because it isn't like he wants me like that anyway," I say, holding my hand out to him. "I mean, look at him. Greek god. Look at that ass, Riana."

She giggles. "Now that you point it out, it's hard to look at anything else."

"Exactly! Then look at me, pudgy, middle-aged mom."

She rolls her eyes so hard I'm worried they'll get lost in the back of her head. "Oh, for the love of God. You just turned thirty-one, and you aren't pudgy, you're curvy."

"Middle-aged, baby," I say simply. "Curvy is what skinny girls say to fat girls to make them feel better."

"They do not!" she says, throwing her hands up. "You're so dramatic."

Smacking her, I laugh, but before I can tell her to shut up, I hear, "I've been saying that for years."

Ugh. Simon's voice makes my skin crawl. Kaia is on his arm.

Riana, always her lovely self, makes a face. "No one is talking to you."

"Ah, don't be mean, little sis. I came to say hi. Look at you, all big and glowing."

She glares before looking over at me. "I can't stab him, can I?"

I shake my head. "He's the boys' father."

"Small complications," she says before crossing her arms and looking at the field. I want to do the same, but before I can, he says, "So funny story." I doubt it's gonna be funny at all, but I listen as he goes on. "Kaia told me about the man at your house when she came to pick the boys up—"

"Did she tell you she came extremely early? I had just walked into the house. Next time, call."

He ignores me, going on. "And I was like, wow, that's good. She's moving on, but then we find out you hired him to nanny our boys."

Riana turns in her seat, glaring up at him. "So? You aren't helping in any way."

"Doesn't matter. I'm their father."

"So? He's a good guy, a friend of Phillip's."

"So? I didn't hire him."

"Well, that's because you can't sleep with him," she snaps, and I lay my hand on hers.

Bless her, but she doesn't know how to control her mouth around Simon. Not that I can blame her. "Riana, go over with Phillip."

She glares as Simon just laughs. "Yeah, go on, little sis."

"Are you sure I can't at least kick him?"

Simon's laughter sets my teeth on edge as I shake my head. "Just go."

When she stands, I do too, folding my arms across my chest as I turn to him. "I hired nine different nannies, and none of them worked. So far so good with Lincoln."

"But it isn't right. At least to me it's not. I'm not okay with it. He's Phillip's friend, right? The guy from the other night."

Ugh, I should have told him earlier. I point to Lincoln, who was standing with Phillip, but then I see him striding over.

Holding out his hand to Simon, he says, "Hey, I'm Lincoln Scott. We met the other night, but I don't think we've met properly. I'm the one caring for the boys when Vera is at work."

Simon looks up at him before looking at me, ignoring Lincoln's hand. "No way."

"It isn't your decision. I'm paying for him," I say simply.

Simon's eyes almost come out of his head. "He's a man! What if he—"

"I can send you every single one of his recommendations. If you ask the boys, they respect him. We need that. I don't think you realize how bad we need that for the boys. They haven't respected anyone, but they respect him. He is a great caregiver, and I don't care what you have to say about it."

"They're great kids—"

But Simon cuts Lincoln off, like the jackass he is. "I know. I am their father."

My temper starts to boil. "And I am their mother. I don't want them going to the school you've chosen, but because they somewhat like it, I don't fight you on it."

"It's a good school," says Simon.

"He's a great nanny."

"Fine, we'll go to court over it, then."

"Jesus, is that all you do? Throw that at me? I'm not scared of you, Simon," I say, my voice rising. That is until Lincoln's hand comes to the small of my back. Breathing heavily, I look over at him, meeting his heated gaze.

"Charlie is within ear shot, and while I get your ex is a douche, I don't think you want to upset your son."

"A douche? You don't know me, kid. I can ruin you."

"Jesus Christ," I mutter, exhaling hard as I look at Riana trying to talk to Charlie so he can't see. "We can discuss this later."

"I'd love to see you try," Lincoln says.

That surprises me. This isn't his fight; he doesn't even have a dog in it. Well, except his job, but he doesn't know this man from Adam, and in a way, I feel like he is trying to protect me.

I don't think Simon even notices. He says, "Or you can just agree to let me take the boys for spring break, and I'll let it go."

"Oh, go fuck yourself, Simon," I say simply. "Honestly—"

"Mom, you good?"

Charlie's voice stops me, and I press my lips together. Lincoln moves his hand along my back soothingly.

"Yes, love. I'm fine."

Charlie doesn't seem convinced before he says, "You look upset. Are you two really fighting during Louis and Elliot's game?"

"No, not at all," I say, reaching for him and squeezing his hand three times. "No worries."

He eyes me and then his father before shaking his head. "Leave her alone, Dad. Go back to the bleachers."

"We're just talking, son—"

"I don't care. She was happy before you got here."

Charlie's eyes cut to Lincoln's, and I don't miss the way he nods to my boy. With that, Charlie turns, heading back to where Riana and Phillip are standing. Riana wraps her arms around Charlie, kissing his cheek, and of course, he tries to get away, but she doesn't let him get far. I smile and take a cleansing breath. I feel Lincoln looking at me, and when I turn my face just a bit, he's there, his eyes on me. "Wanna go over with them?"

"I do," I say softly, and he gives me a weak smile. Nodding his head, he presses into my back, urging me toward them, but I pause, looking back at Simon. "We can discuss this another time when our children aren't around. Excuse me."

I want to be giddy over the fact that Lincoln is touching me, but Simon ruins that within seconds. "So easy for you to walk away when this is serious, Vera. I'm not joking. I don't want him to watch our children."

I just shrug. "I'll see you in court, then."

And I'm not lying. I am over it. I won't keep fighting, especially when it was my job to find a caregiver. I am paying for him—that is that. I refuse to allow him to think he can threaten me with court. I have been a victim of his for too long. Not anymore.

Now, I choose to be happy.

Just as we reach Riana, Phillip, and Charlie, Lincoln's hand falls from my waist, and I wish it hadn't. It felt right there. But Charlie is looking at me, so I know Lincoln not touching me is for the best. "Are you okay?"

"I'm fine, love," I say, squeezing his hand, but he doesn't look convinced. I want to reassure him, but my time is up when the whistle is blown. The twins' game is over, which means they'll all leave with Simon. I bite into my cheek as I pull Charlie in close, kissing his cheek and ignoring his groans. When I'm tackled by two little boys, I smile as I wrap my arms around their sweaty necks. "You guys did great! I love watching you two play together."

Elliot's eyes go wide. "Coach says we're unstoppable!"

"You are!" Lincoln and I say together, and then we share a small smile before I cup Louis's face.

"Your goal was sick," I say.

His face lights up so much it takes my breath away. Or maybe it's the stench they are putting off.

"But you two smell disgusting," I groan, even though I'm met with laughter.

Louis hugs me tightly. "We don't want to leave you."

"I know—"

"Boys, let's go," Simon calls.

I don't miss the way Charlie glares at him. I cup his face. "Be nice. Be good, all of you."

"We will," the twins chime, but Charlie makes no such promise.

Kissing all three of their heads, I tell them I love them before they say bye to everyone else and then run off with my ex-husband. I let out a long sigh and wish like hell they weren't leaving. When Phillip's arm slings across my neck, I look up at him as he smiles down at me. "Don't worry. I'll get you drunk, and you won't think a bit about that fucker."

"What?" Riana says, coming to my other side. "She has a date tonight."

"She does?"

They both look to me, and then I even feel Lincoln looking at me.

I clear my throat, my face turning red. "I canceled."

"What! You puss!"

I laugh at my sister's teasing tone. "I wasn't ready for it."

She yells something as she reaches for her bag, which is beside our chairs, but all I hear is Lincoln say, "I think it was the right choice."

I meet his gaze, taken back by his words. His lips curve, and I'm utterly confused by him.

I want him.

I'm not sure if he wants me.

As Lincoln helps Phillip gather all our things, I watch as Riana comes up beside me, a little kitten grin on her face.

"So I heard we're going to dinner with Lincoln," she sings.

I roll my eyes. "To get to know him."

"Yeah, but nothing says you can't take him home and..." Her words trail off as she runs to her husband and takes hold of his hips before humping him as he's bent over. "All night long."

"Riana! What the hell?" Phillip complains, but I'm the one bent over laughing as she continues to assault her husband. "What in the world are you doing?"

"Demonstration, jeez," she complains, smacking his butt. "Most men love when their wives do that."

Wheezing, I say, "Oh, my God, you're a nut."

She beams over at me as Phillip gives her a confused look. "Hump their ass? I don't think so." He looks at Lincoln, who's laughing and shaking his head. "Do you like that?"

Lincoln swallows his laughter, lifting one of the chairs up under his arm. "If it's the right woman, why not?"

I swear his gaze meets mine in a quick but very naughty way. It's only for a second before he grabs the other chair.

But it has me breathless.

"Holy shit. I saw that," Riana says under her breath to me.

I look to Riana with wide eyes. "See!"

"You're totally getting laid tonight."

"Please."

"No, it's happening."

"Riana!"

"Nope, leave it to me!"

"Riana!" I holler even louder, but she's off taking her husband's hand and swinging it happily.

I know I'm in trouble.

I should be scared, right?

Right.

So why I am excited?

# CHAPTER NINE

## LINCOLN

"So they're running, and when I say running, I mean like sprinting across this field." Phillip pauses to laugh as he shakes his head.

Across the table, the girls are giggling—well Riana is, but Vera is hiding her mouth as she snorts with laughter. I love the way her eyes are sparkling. She's stunning.

"And of course, this was when I was overweight, so I was struggling to catch up. I turn the corner, and they're gone. Legit, gone. Apparently they were hiding in a hole!"

"A hole?" I laugh, and Vera snorts.

Riana's head falls back, laughter shaking her body. "We had to get away," she chortles, and I can't help but laugh harder.

Phillip gives her a deadpan look. "Yeah, thanks. So of course, I go to jail."

"You didn't go to jail!" Vera insists. "He was in holding until he gave us up."

"Which I wouldn't!"

Riana giggles. "So we sent our uncle, who is a lawyer, to get him. He was traumatized. Until it happened again. Then I think he got used to it."

I laugh as I lean back in the plush chair. "It happened again?"

"The next week!" Phillip complains, which just sends them into a fit of laughter again. "I swear to God, I don't know what it is with them and their hometown officer, but he was out to catch them."

"What in the world did you do?"

"Trespassing."

"Skinny dipping," Riana added, counting off her fingers.

"Wasn't there an assault?" asks Vera. "I don't remember. I was drunk."

Riana scoffed. "You knocked Simon upside the head with a loaf of bread, and he called the sheriff."

Phillip snorted. "And dude, that cop showed up and Vera was gone. Hiding in the trunk of my car."

I try to hold in my laughter, but I can't. "I don't believe it."

Vera nods, still laughing. "Oh, I was rotten."

"We both were," Riana adds between snorts.

"Which is why we haven't been back there in what, ten years?" Vera asks, holding her wine to her lips.

If anyone were to ask, I am staring at the glass, not the lips.

Which is the biggest lie of the night.

I'm actually staring at her lips and then her jaw and her neck and then those lavish breasts. Today she's wearing jeans that hug her so tightly my mouth is watering at the sight of her. Along with the shirt that clings to her waist and breasts, I'm surprised my dish towel stayed in place earlier today.

She's absolutely stunning.

And with each passing second I spend with her, I'm

regretting my promise to my best friend.

"We'd go back, and I swear they wouldn't recognize us," Vera says.

"Especially you! But really, has it been ten? Yeah, the last time we went, you found out you were pregnant with the twins."

She nodded. "Simon proposed a little after that."

"Even after you slapped him with a loaf of bread," Phillip says.

She scoffs. "It was Bunny Bread. It hardly hurt."

"I don't know... You swung that really hard."

Riana snorted. "Then threw each slice in his face."

Phillip choked on his laughter. "I just remember him saying, 'Stop, this is assault. It hurts.' He was such a bitch."

"Was? Still is," Vera says, shaking her head, obviously lost in the distant memory.

Holding my hand up, I say, "I'm confused. First, I didn't know I was hanging with convicts." Both women hoot at that. "How'd you guys end up here?"

Riana looks at Vera just as she does the same. With a small smile, she looks back to me before saying, "When we lost our parents, our dad's mom was the one to get custody of us. Well, more so Riana, since I was almost eighteen, but that didn't matter 'cause she wasn't going anywhere without me."

"Or she without me," Riana says with a grin. "But we ended up here, and we never left. Simon's punk-ass moved here to be closer to Charlie, and our grandma helped him get a job with our uncle. So he actually wouldn't be where he is without our family."

"She's bitter," Vera jokes, sending her sister a grin, and I smile. "But she isn't wrong."

"Not at all," Phillip adds, and we all laugh then as our meals are brought out.

Since I notice everything Vera does, I watch as she taps her glass, quietly asking for another as Riana throws mushrooms on Phillip's plate.

I smile. "That's insane."

"Yeah, we were wild, but we've calmed down a lot," Vera says, looking to her sister lovingly.

"You have. Riana hasn't," Phillip decides.

Riana smacks him playfully. "I am a model citizen."

"You're just smart and don't get caught," Vera says then, and Riana glares over at her, sticking her tongue out. She laughs once more and then downs the rest of her drink as everyone's laughter subsides. I like this part of her. The joking part. It's amazing to see her smile so much.

When she clears her throat, I look up and she says, "You two were friends, right? Met in college?"

I nod. "We met in high school, but yeah, went to college together and even lived together."

Phillip scoffs. "You should have seen it, Vera. My dad gave us the ultimate pad."

"Despite my mother's wishes." I laugh, and he grins over at me.

"Oh, really?" Vera asks.

Riana nods. "Phillip's dad told them not to do anything but go to school. Apparently, they did everything but go to school."

I laugh as I shake my head. "Excuse me. I went."

"I'm sorry. Lincoln went while Phillip almost flunked out freshman year."

Vera's eyes widen. "Phillip! Really?"

He shrugs. "Hey, I was a fucked-up kid."

I raise my glass. "Truth."

"But he found his way," Riana said softly, moving her hand with his.

"Or he found a great piece of ass he couldn't give up, and she molded him into the perfect man," I tease, and I'm rewarded with a middle finger as Vera snorts with laughter, holding her hand over her face.

"You made wine come out of my nose!" she complains, and I laugh before handing her a napkin. Phillip and Riana joining in.

"Serves you right. You shouldn't be drinking anyway."

Vera makes a face. "Why? I'm not driving. Phillip is."

Phillip gives her a deadpan look. "Thanks, Vera."

"What? Wait, no, you're driving, Riana."

She rolls her eyes. "Whatever."

I chuckle as I take a long pull of my glass, but when I set it down, she reaches over and takes it. "What the hell!"

"You're driving," Riana says simply. "And it's your third."

"Fourth, and I can handle my drink."

"No, I need you to make it home," she says before handing my drink to Vera, who sends me a wide grin before taking a pull of my beer.

"I didn't take you as a beer drinker."

Looking at me from over the mug, she smiles. "I'm an anything drinker."

"Amen," Phillip jokes, but Riana doesn't find any of us funny. She looks upset, but then the waitress sets down her baked potato, and she's happy again.

Pregnancy hormones. Gah.

"So you were born and raised here. Ever going to leave?"

I just took a bite of my steak, so chewing around it, I say, "Nope. I love it here."

"But you were gonna go to Germany, weren't you?"

I swallow my bite as I nod. "I was, but I knew it wouldn't be forever."

"Do you still talk to that family?"

I smile. "I do, daily."

"Wow."

"I miss them a lot."

"Yeah, but I'm glad you didn't go," Phillip adds, taking a pull of his beer. "I'd miss you."

"Aww," Riana and Vera tease, but he doesn't pay them any mind.

"Hey, he's my brother from another mother."

Riana rolls her eyes, but I find myself feeling a bit of guilt. I made a promise, but I haven't been sticking to it. I flirted with Vera today, a lot, and if she even showed any kind of interest, I would have kissed her. My hand is still burning from touching her earlier. She's so warm, so beautiful, and I've never wanted to protect someone the way I wanted to protect her. It's been a long while since I wanted to fight a man, but I wouldn't mind beating the shit out of Simon.

He is a douche.

"You know he is going to get married one day," Riana says

then, distracting me from my thoughts. "He won't be with you forever."

I smile as Phillip shrugs. "Yes, but I got married, and we're still the best of friends."

"For the love of God, you're drunk."

"Leave him alone, Ri. You're jealous," I tease, and she sticks her tongue out at me playfully.

"Fine, maybe a bit," she says, but Phillip leans into her, kissing the side of her mouth.

"Nothing to be jealous of. You're my number one."

"I'm number zero," I tease and she glares, but then her mouth is busy with Phillip, which gives me the perfect opportunity to grab my beer. But when I do, Vera does at the same time, our hands crashing together. Her eyes widen as she looks back at me, and I send her a quick wink before reaching for it to down most of it. Impressed, she claps her hands quietly, and I laugh before setting it back in front of her plate.

She's fun.

Holding my gaze, she moves her fork through her spaghetti.

"Is it not good?" I ask.

She shakes her head quickly. "No, it's fabulous. I just keep wondering how our paths never crossed before. I remember hearing Phillip and the boys say 'Linc,' but I guess I was always so busy, I just didn't pay attention."

My lip quirks as I shrug. "Yeah, I guess, but you know, they did cross once."

Her brows shoot up. "Huh? When?"

"Yeah, when?" Riana asks, confused. "I didn't know that.

Did you?"

"No," Phillip says simply.

I just smile. "I mean, not really, but I was sleeping off a hangover one morning at their house, and you had come over to get something—I don't remember. But Riana had asked for you to keep it down, and you said, I quote, 'I'm not keeping my voice down 'cause some asshole doesn't know how to handle his liquor.'"

Her face turns beet red as a guilty smile curves her lips.

It is honestly the most gorgeous thing I have ever seen.

Covering her mouth, she looks to Riana. "I did do that."

"You did!" she gasps, pointing to her sister and laughing. "Jesus, that was eons ago! Weren't you pregnant with the twins?"

"I think so."

"I don't remember this," Phillip says.

Riana slaps the table as she laughs. "'Cause you were on the floor passed out beside him! I had picked y'all up from some party."

Phillip goes back to eating. "That makes sense."

"It does," I agree.

Vera glances back at me. "Sorry?"

I wave her off. "No need. It was so long ago."

"I was angry and pregnant."

"Hey, I'm not judging," I say, holding up a hand. She grins, and a blush settles along her cheeks. I want so badly to tell her she is beautiful. That she is way too good for that bastard Simon. That I'd like to take her by that sweet face of hers and kiss the living shit out of her.

But I made a promise.

Fucking promise.

"Well, let's make a toast." Phillip holds up his glass, and I reach for my beer, causing Vera to laugh a bit as Riana glares at me. "To new beginnings. To getting to know each other and long-lasting relationships. Oh, and to the boys, Charlie, Louis, and Elliot. May they always feel loved and needed."

Vera sighs happily, which is innocent enough, but apparently my cock doesn't know that. For that simple sound has me harder than a rock as we clank our glasses together, all repeating, "To the boys."

Which is the reason I am here.

Because I am the manny.

And she's my boss.

I really need to keep reminding myself of that.

# CHAPTER TEN

## LINCOLN

Once we finish dinner and settle the tab, we gather our things to head out. It was a great night, a great day actually, and I'm glad Phillip invited me, though I'm pretty sure he did with the intentions of Vera and me getting to know each other. While that had happened, it also made my crush on Vera stronger. I enjoyed watching her eat and laugh—man, I love her laugh. Her smile, though, is the best, and not her fake smile but her real one. The one that lights up her eyes and makes the little lines by them show.

Yup, clearly I have it bad for my boss.

But apparently no one knows of my struggles, for when we arrive in the parking lot, Riana asks, "Hey, Lincoln, why don't you run Vera home?"

Phillip's brows pull together, and I don't miss the pure panic on Vera's face as she eyes Riana. Phillip looks down at his wife, asking, "What, why?"

"'Cause I want to go home," she coos, running her fingers along his chest.

Within seconds, gone is Phillip's confusion. "Yes, take her home, Linc, please."

"Wow, thanks!" Vera calls to them.

"Hey, I gotta get it in before this kid comes and I don't get it at all," he says, and Riana smacks him, but they're both laughing, grabbing each other as they go toward their car. I'm taken by them. They are completely and utterly in love, and it does nothing but leave me envious as hell.

I want that.

I had my fair share of relationships, but no one ever did what Riana does for Phillip. Complete him. I want that. But I can't help but think I'll never find it if I'm in fact taking care of other families instead of finding someone to make my own.

Or maybe I already found her but I can't have her.

Silence falls around me.

Vera glances up at me shyly as she shrugs. "I can call an Uber."

"Nonsense. I'll take you home. It's on the way."

"Are you sure?"

"Absolutely, unless you want to ride home with someone else."

Her eyes turn such a dark color as she slowly shakes her head. "I don't."

"Cool, then let's go." I reach for her, pressing my hand into the middle of her back as we head toward my SUV. I'm getting comfortable doing that, and I'm not sure what that means. I shouldn't be touching her, but I can't stop myself.

Which is probably against all the rules of that promise I made.

And I should probably care more...

I'm a horrible friend.

Opening the door for her, I help her in since it's so high off the ground.

"I bet the boys love this thing."

"Oh, yeah, they do," I say, and she chuckles as I shut the door before rushing around it to get in myself. I turn the car on, hitting the heat and then bundling up in my thin jacket. "Damn, it's chilly tonight."

"It is. I wish I had brought a coat."

"Do you want mine?"

She scoffs. "I'm fine."

I eye her. "Why'd you make that noise?"

Her brows pull together. "What noise?"

"That noise of 'please, yeah right.'"

"Did I?" She chuckles.

I nod. "Yeah."

She looks away, her laughter dying down. "It's just silly to think your jacket would fit me."

"Why wouldn't it?"

She eyes me. "Really?"

I give her a look. "What? Don't be weird. Jeez," I say, taking my jacket off and handing it to her. "Put it on."

"I'm really fine."

"No, put it on," I demand, and her eyes narrow a bit as if she wants to argue with me. Instead, though, a grin pulls at her lips. Slowly, her eyes never leaving mine, she puts on my jacket. I have to say, it's the first time I've ever begged a woman to put on clothes. My jacket actually drowns her, like I knew it would. "See."

She cuddles into it. "Okay."

"Okay, what?"

"You were right."

"Say it again, louder for the people in the back." Her glare deepens, and my grin doesn't falter. "Ready?"

"Yeah."

I'm met with a grin that hits me straight in the gut. As I pull out of the parking lot, I find that I'm nervous, which is odd. What the hell do I have to be nervous about? I just have the hottest chick I've ever seen in my life riding shotgun, and it's fantastic because I can't touch her.

I promised my best friend.

And she's my boss.

See, nothing to be nervous about.

Annoyed with myself, I reach for the tunes and turn it up. "You like music, right?"

She gives me a deadpan look. "Duh."

"Just making sure." I laugh as the radio blasts the newest Justin Timberlake. When her eyes widen a bit, I wonder why. "Are you a fan?"

"I am."

"Me too. Good body-rubbing music."

Her face fills with color, and I can't stop grinning. It's fun flirting with her, though I don't think she realizes I am. "Body-rubbing music?"

I show her all my teeth in a grin. "Yup."

She just giggles, shaking her head as the music plays. Soon we're both singing along together, and of course, I start dancing to the music. Growing up with all girls through the Backstreet Boys and New Kids on the Block era, it's easy to say I was in a lot of dance-offs. But it's different with Vera than with my sisters.

She has a nice voice, but when she adds in her amazing dance moves, I am finding it hard to breathe.

"I can't with you. The sprinkler? It's almost twenty-twenty!"

She laughs. "Hey, the sprinkler will never get old!"

"Touché, touché!"

"All you keep doing is thrusting."

"I'm driving!"

"True, don't kill us. Riana would be pissed."

"She would. Probably kill me again."

"Exactly."

"She's insane."

"She's the best, though."

"She is," I agree, and when I chance a glance, she's smiling. Of course, seeing that smile only makes me grin wider and want to kiss the hell out of her. It's short–lived, though, since when I turn onto her street, my heart sinks.

I don't want this to end.

I hadn't expected for that feeling to rush up on me like this. I know I enjoy looking at her, but I'm also finding that I love being around her.

She's the total package.

Not wanting to let her get out, I say, "So the boys come home tomorrow?"

Her smile grows a bit, but I see a lot of nervousness in it. "Yeah, at seven. Hopefully Simon stays in the car."

"Do you want me to come over?"

She waves me off. "It's fine. I've been dealing with him way longer than I care to admit."

"So it's never been good?" I ask just as I pull into her drive. "Well, I guess not, since you threw bread at him."

"And a baseball bat."

My eyes widen. "What?"

"I used to be very passionate about him."

I smile. "So you being passionate is throwing baseball bats?"

"Hey, no one said I was perfect."

I laugh as she smiles.

"But not all of it was bad, if that makes any sense," she says softly. "He has always been a wonderful dad."

"Really?"

"Yeah, he loves the boys, very much. I guess he just never loved me."

I don't know what to say, but then I mutter, "Well, he's an idiot."

Her eyes widen a bit as she glances up at me through her lashes. "That is the damn truth."

We share a smile, but when she goes to take off my jacket, I stop her. "Keep it. I'll grab it when I come over Monday."

She smiles a thanks, but when I shut off the car, her eyes widen. "Are you coming in?"

I wiggle my brows at her. "Do you want me too?"

Her lips part, and this look of pure humiliation covers her face as her mouth moves but no words come out. She does that a lot around me, and all I can do is laugh. Because I'd kiss her if I didn't laugh.

"I'm going to walk you to the door, Vera. Relax." I get out and go around to help her out, but she's already shutting the door when I reach her. "Jerk. I'm supposed to help you out. Be a gentleman and all that."

She scoffs. "Pretty sure a gentleman doesn't call a lady a jerk."

I press my lips together. "You're right on that. Please don't tell my mom."

I'm answered with her giggles as we walk around the SUV and up the front path. "Secret is safe with me."

My body is tingling for her as we walk in silence. I want to reach out, take her hand in mine, and then pull her closer for our mouths to meet. I want to tell her that this is the best date ever, and it isn't even a date. I want to take her up the stairs to her room and lay her down on that massive bed of hers.

I want a lot of things I know I can't have.

Reaching the front door, she searches her purse for her keys as she says, "I'm good. You don't have to wait. It's chilly tonight."

"No way. Riana would kill me if I didn't make sure you got in okay." She sends me a grin as she digs in the bottom of her purse. I look up at the house and then glance back to her. "Can I ask you something?"

"Sure," she says, just as she finds her keys.

"How do you afford this house? It's huge!"

She laughs as she pushes the door open. "I bought it with my inheritance from my parents."

"Oh. So it's paid off, then?"

She grins. "It is, you nosey ass."

I laugh. "Yeah, I guess that is rude. Don't tell my mom I said that either."

She leans into the door. "I guess when I meet your mama, we won't have much to say."

"Oh, she'll have plenty. She talks more than anyone I know."

Her eyes brighten a bit as she looks me over. "Are you heading home?"

Tucking my hands into my pockets, I nod. "I am."

She inhales hard, her eyes burning into mine, and when she looks at me like that, I lose all train of thought. "Do you want to come in for a glass of wine?"

I'm not sure if she really wants me to come in for a glass of wine or if it is code for having my way with her, but I know if I go in there, I'll do the latter.

And I can't do that.

Biting into my lip, I move my head toward my car. "I gotta go. I have an early morning."

"Oh?"

"Yeah, I go to church with my family on Sundays."

Her eyes widen as she laughs softly. "So let me get this straight," she says, holding up her hand before counting off each finger. "You clean, cook, do laundry, care for kids, and go to church on Sundays? Oh, and you love your mom."

And some would say I fuck like a dream, but I know I can't say that, so I smile. "I do."

"Are you sure you're not gay?"

"Oh, Vera, if only I could show you—" I pause, swallowing hard as I hold her gaze. My whole body is on fire. I want more than anything to press her into that door and show her all of me, but apparently I have the restraint of a saint. I clear my throat and say, "How very not gay I am."

Her lips part before she pulls in a deep breath, and all I want is to kick myself. I am turning down this beautiful woman, like an idiot. "Good night, Vera."

"Night, Lincoln."

Turning from her, I swear I'll never regret anything more than the moment when I walked away from a very wanton Vera.

But, hey, I kept my promise.

That makes me a good person.

Even though I really want to be bad.

Very bad.

# CHAPTER ELEVEN

## LINCOLN

After Saturday, I was finding it an absolute struggle to be around Vera.

On one hand, I had my promise to my best friend, and on the other, I had this undeniable need for her. I want to believe that she too has a need for me, but if she did, why hadn't she done anything yet?

*Because she's your boss, you dumbass.*

She's been on my mind twenty-four seven for the last few days, and I wish I could say it's getting easier to deal with, but it isn't. Each day, I swear she gets hotter. I don't know when I became obsessed with business attire, but seeing her each morning, in tight skirts or fitted dress pants, has done nothing but wreak havoc on my heart. I want to slide my hands up the back of her thighs, grab that ass of hers, and whisper how fucking beautiful I think she is.

It's mind-blowing how she moves with such poise. Her life is a mess, and I don't mean that in a shitty way. Honestly, her ex is a douchebag, but she acts as if none of that matters. Only the boys and her work. I am loved by one great mom, but watching Vera with her boys, it knocks me on my ass as envy eats me alive. I want to be on the receiving end of that love, and I know that is insane and pathetic, but it's true. She is so loving, even when Charlie is being a punk, and it's beautiful to see.

I still don't understand how someone would ever leave her.

Moving through the kitchen, getting breakfast ready, I can hear all of them moving upstairs. I have a pan of eggs and some bacon going, per Louis's request. While it's only been a week, I have a groove that works for everyone. I come first thing in the morning, getting everything going in the kitchen while Vera and the boys get ready upstairs. When she leaves, the boys and I eat before heading to school. While they're at school, I do things around here and back at my place, and then I'll go sit with Lincoln to the second power for a bit until I gotta go get the boys. While I'm not making the money I was, I'm really happy.

I hear heels on the stairs and look up from plating the boys' food, waiting for Vera to enter the kitchen. Today she is wearing a dress, one that reaches the ground and hugs her waist tight before flowing out. Her hair is down and so damn luscious, framing her beautiful face.

Glancing over at me, she takes my breath away as she says, "Morning."

"Morning."

She moves around the island before reaching for a coffee cup. "So remember that Charlie has his therapy right after school. They should be getting all their stuff together to bring with them and put in your car."

"Yup, I had it written down and was going to remind them."

"You're awesome," she says, and I beam back at her. "I really appreciate you taking him for me. I hate that I can't take him."

"Yeah, but you get to come home early tomorrow and it's my job."

"This is true," she says simply as she leans into the counter. "I still hate not going."

"I know, but I can tell you everything they tell me."

"Which probably won't be anything, but I want to know what Charlie says, so can you call me after you drop them off at practice?"

"I can," I say, meeting her gaze, and then I smile as I drink in how beautiful she looks. "I like that dress."

Her eyes widen as she looks down at herself. "You do?"

"It looks really good on you."

"I don't look frumpy?"

I shake my head. "Not even close."

Her eyes sparkle as her lips tip. "Well, that's a very nice thing to say. I didn't realize compliments were included in your salary."

My eyes burn into hers. "They're not."

Her grin grows as the twins come barreling down the stairs. I tear my gaze from Vera when the boys come into the kitchen and jump up on the stools ready to eat breakfast. "You guys have everything packed? Elliot, you have that science study guide right?"

He nods eagerly as he stuffs his mouth with bacon. "Yeah, and my language."

"Good. You got everything, Louis?"

"Yup," he says before shoveling eggs into his mouth. These boys can eat.

"Where is Charlie?"

"He's coming," Louis informs me before looking to his mom. "You're working late tonight?"

"Yes, love," she says sadly.

Louis makes a face. "Can't you work late Wednesday so that you can be home to spend time with us before we leave for Dad's?"

I look back to her and see the guilt floating in her eyes.

"I already work late Wednesdays, but let me see what I can do," she says before reaching for his hand, squeezing it. I notice they do that a lot. I'm not sure what it means, but it brings such light to their eyes. She moves to Elliot and kisses his forehead. "I'm gonna head out. You guys have a great day."

"Don't forget your breakfast," I say before she can leave the kitchen.

She glances back at me, a grin starting to pull at her lips. "You made me breakfast?"

I hand her the wrap I made, which is in a napkin. "You gotta eat too."

With a grin that now covers her face, she says, "Well, thank you."

"You're welcome." My voice drops a bit as I hold her gaze. "I'll call you later."

"Thank you, again," she says on an exhale before kissing the boys once more and leaving the kitchen. She calls up to Charlie, but he doesn't call back down, and I watch as her shoulders fall. I think she felt me watching her, for when she looks back at me, she shrugs.

I give her a weak smile and say, "Have a great day."

But she's already heading out the door, obviously upset. I hate how much pressure is on her. I want to take it all away. I want to taste her. I want to hold her, and damn it, I want to make her scream.

Gah, she drives me wild, and she doesn't even realize it.

"I think Dad shouldn't get us every weekend."

I look to Louis. "No?"

"No, it's not fair. Mom doesn't get to spend any time with us on the weekends."

"Maybe she can take a day off during the week?" Elliot asks.

I shrug. "I don't know. You'll have to ask her."

"Yeah, I guess," Elliot says, and I can tell he is upset by this. They love their mom. They want to spend time with her, and I don't blame them. I want to too.

Glancing at the clock, I make a face. Charlie should have been down here by now. Tapping the island, I point to the boys. "Want more before I go and round up your brother?"

"Yes," Louis says.

I point to the pan. "Get it, then, but don't burn yourself."

As he gets up, I head into the living room and stop at the bottom of the stairs. "Hey, Charlie, breakfast is ready."

He doesn't answer me at first, but then I hear, "I'm good."

I make a face. "You need to eat. Come on down."

"I'm not feeling good."

Huh. I take the stairs two at a time and then walk down the hall. I still don't understand how Vera has pictures up of

Simon. She's stronger than I am, but when I asked, she said it is to keep things as normal as she can for the boys.

Good woman right there.

I would have burned the photos.

Reaching his room, I knock on the door before I push it open.

Charlie is on the floor, playing Xbox, still in his PJs. Glancing back at me, he groans. "I don't want to go to school. I don't feel good."

He looks just fine to me. "What's wrong?"

"My stomach hurts."

"Probably 'cause you're hungry."

"No, I just don't feel good. I want to stay home."

"Okay, well, you look fine to me."

He looks back at me once more. "You don't know my body."

I shrug. "I don't, but I know you're fine enough to play games."

His eyes narrow, looking a lot like Vera as he gazes up at me. "I don't want to go."

"Fine. You know you still have to go to therapy, and then you won't go to practice."

His brows pull together. "You can't do that. I have to go to practice."

I shake my head. "If you don't feel well enough to go to school, you're not well enough to go to practice."

His eyes fill with anger. "That's bullshit."

"Whoa, man," I say, holding my hands up. "Have I used language like that with you?"

He doesn't answer, just glares.

"Let me answer for you—no, I haven't. So don't use it with me. Get dressed, come down, and eat. Make sure you have your stuff so we can go to practice straight from therapy."

"Whatever."

Ah, to be a teenager again.

Heading out of the room, I find the twins standing in the hall with their eyes wide. I smile. "You guys good?"

They nod quickly before going into the bathroom to brush their teeth. Shaking my head, I head down the stairs, and just as I reach the bottom one, my phone rings. It's Vera.

"Hey."

"Did you tell Charlie he can't go to practice if he doesn't go to school?"

"I did," I say, kicking the bottom of the stairs. I can't believe that kid told on me. "Is that a problem?"

She pauses. "He says he doesn't feel well."

"He's fine, Vera." I head into the kitchen. "I don't think he wants to go to therapy."

She inhales deeply, and then there's silence. Suddenly, she says, "Okay."

"Okay?"

"Yeah, I trust you."

"You sure?"

I'm met with laughter that has no humor in it. "No, yes, I don't know. I'm just nervous. I worry so much that he'll go back and tell Simon something, but I know that I can't live like that, that I have to raise him the way I always have. I've been feeling so guilty lately."

I nod, though she can't see me. "That's understandable, but Vera, you're a wonderful mom."

She scoffs. "My boys want me home, and I can't even give them that."

"You are doing your best."

"It should be better," she says softly.

I shake my head. "I think you're doing awesome."

"You're just being nice."

"I'm being honest," I insist and hope that makes her feel a little better. "I do think that maybe you should see about getting one weekend to be with the boys."

She exhales loudly. "I've already decided I'm going to talk to my lawyer today. I'm just worried that doing that will bring attention on you, and I can't have that. I need you."

Ah, if only she *needed* me in the bedroom.

*You are a dirty man, Lincoln Scott! She is being honest with you, and you're thinking of sex!*

I'm pathetic.

"Yeah," I say softly. "And if they ask Charlie right now, he may hate me."

She laughs. "I'm sure he doesn't."

"Hopefully. I'll talk to him." I smile as I scoop up some of the eggs Elliot left behind. "Don't worry. Everything will be okay."

"Thank you."

"Anytime. I'll talk to you later?"

"Yeah," she says, and then the line goes dead.

As I clean, I replay our conversation. I want so desperately to fix this for her. Problem is, I can't. I have no horse in this race, but I want one.

I want her.

Jesus, I am setting myself up for failure left and right.

When I hear someone coming down the stairs, I finish wrapping up some eggs and bacon for Charlie as he enters the kitchen dressed and ready. He glares at me as he sits down, and I hand him his wrap. I don't say anything as he starts to eat before I pour him some orange juice. When I set it in front of him, I ask, "Wanna tell me what's going on?" He doesn't answer, just chews as he looks at his plate. Bending down, I look at his face. His brows are furrowed, and he looks as if he wants to hurt something. Or someone. "You know you gotta go to school, bud."

He exhales hard as he pulls his beanie down a little over his eyes, ignoring me completely. In other words, he just told me to fuck off. Shrugging my shoulders, I start to clean as the twins move around upstairs. I can hear them running and yelling at each other to grab things. We have to leave in a bit, but we're not hurting on time. I want Charlie to talk to me, but I know I can't push him. He's got to do it on his own time. I just hope he realizes that I'm here for him.

As I wipe down the counter, I hear him moving as he puts his plate and cup in the sink. I look over at him, and say, "Thanks."

He looks at me, his eyes dark as he shrugs. "No problem. It was good."

"Good, I'm glad you liked it." Charlie looks away, and I lean back into the counter, balling up the rag I was holding. "You know you can talk to me."

He doesn't look at me as he shrugs. "I just don't want to go."

"Why?" When he shrugs again, I notice his shoulders are taut and he looks on edge. "Are kids still messing with you?"

He shakes his head quickly. "No, that stopped."

"Well, that's good."

"Yeah," he agrees as he toes the hardwood with his sneaker. "My dad texted me, saying he is coming to lunch with me today. I told him I didn't want him to, but he said he needs to talk to me."

Well, shit. Clearing my throat, I ask, "Why don't you want him to?"

"'Cause I know what he wants to talk about."

"Do you want to tell me what that is?"

He shakes his head. "He wants me to talk to my mom about spring break so that he and Kaia can take us on vacation, but I know Mom would want to go with us. He's already convinced Elliot and Louis that they want to go, but they won't say anything, so he wants me to."

My heart sinks. How dare this fucker put this kid in the middle. "Do you want to go?"

"I do, but I don't want to hurt my mom. She already doesn't get to see us as much as she wants."

I slowly nod. "So tell him that."

"I have, but he won't listen to me." He looks up at me. "I'm being stupid. I hate all this."

"You're not, but bud, I think you should talk to your mom."

He rolls his eyes. "She's so busy, and I hate to make her worry."

"Yeah, I get that, but if you talk to her about this, I think she'd be able to make it better. She is pretty awesome."

Charlie's lips curve as he nods. "She's the best."

I smile back at him as I grasp his shoulder. "Talk to your mom, and tell your dad that you aren't comfortable talking to him about this. If he wants to have lunch with you, cool, that's good. You should repair your relationship with him—"

"You sound like my therapist."

I laugh. "I grew up with six girls. I know how to talk about my feelings."

He makes a face. "And you survived?"

"Somehow," I joke, and he grins. "But seriously, bud, you can't shut down."

He nods. "I know. It's just easier."

"I hear you on that," I say, squeezing his shoulder. "But I know your mom would love to help you."

"I know."

"So talk to her."

"I will," he says, nodding his head, and a little light is back in his eyes. "Maybe tonight when she gets home."

"Sounds like a plan."

He looks down, inhaling hard. "Thanks, Lincoln."

I pat his back as the boys start down the stairs, and when he looks up to me, I smile. "I'm always here for you."

A small smile fills his face as he nods, but I worry he doesn't believe me. I feel for him. He's such a good kid who's in a shitty situation, and as much as I want to help Vera, I want to help him. Elliot and Louis, too. I want to fix it all, but I know I can't. All I can do is be there for them and try to make some things easier.

But I want so much more.
Shit, I am falling for them.
The one thing I had said I wouldn't do.

# CHAPTER TWELVE

## VERA

After my chat with Richard this morning, some of the weight of the world is off my shoulders. He agreed to let me leave earlier a few days a week so I could see the boys before Simon picks them up, and he refused my offer of working weekends to make up for it. I hadn't expected it to go so well, which means talking to Simon would be awful. Entering my office, I go right for my desk before sitting down and reaching for my phone. My mind has been going a mile a minute all morning. Between the boys wanting me home and then the trouble with Charlie, I am holding on by a string. I just want everything to be normal for us, but I am finding we don't have a normal, and I just have to accept that. So instead, I have to fix everything so my boys can be happy. They're right—I'm not home enough, and I already lost my husband. I can't lose my boys too.

As I dial Simon's number, I can't help but think of Lincoln. It's nothing new; I do this often, but I am so thankful for him. He is doing everything I wanted, and he's doing it like the pro I was told he is. I don't know how or even why I trust him completely. I'm just getting to know him, but sometimes I feel like I've known him my whole life. It's just easy, and he's smart, funny, and it helps that he's gorgeous as hell. But that doesn't matter, because he loves my kids, and he is doing everything I could ever ask. Things I can't do, and while I'm jealous of that, I'm also thankful.

Riana is right.

Darn it.

More of a reason I can't ever act on these unreal feelings I have for him. Ever since Saturday, I have been utterly entrapped by him. I find myself thinking of him in that towel or the way our hands touched when we were at dinner. How he held me when he walked me to the car. I want to believe he feels what I feel, but if that were the case, he wouldn't have turned me down when I asked him inside. He's confusing as fuck, especially when he complimented my dress this morning.

It's just all so confusing, but it has to be this way. If I knew he wanted me the way I want him, I wouldn't be able to stop myself.

And that could ruin everything.

Just as the sound of Simon's voice ruins my morning.

"To what do I owe this call?"

Ugh, he makes my skin crawl. "Hey, I wanted to discuss a few things, and maybe we can talk without arguing."

"I doubt it, but go ahead."

I swear he makes me stabby. "I'm hopeful," I express before going on. "I wanted to discuss with you about maybe working it out to where I get a weekend with the boys."

"No."

I close my eyes. "Reason being is because I work, they have practice, and when I get home, we're doing homework and settling down for the night. I don't remember the last time I took them to the movies or to dinner."

"Not my fault. Cut back on work."

I press my lips together. "I am, but I can't too much because I need to make money. I'm paying for club, for their equipment, for the nanny—"

"Who I don't approve of."

"Simon, please. He is honestly the best thing for the boys—"

"It's only been a week. You don't know that."

"But I do," I insist. "Please, Simon, don't fight me on this."

"I will because I don't want another man with my children. I am their father."

"And no one doubts that, at all. You are a good father, Simon, but Lincoln is a wonderful nanny, and he isn't replacing you."

He scoffs. "So you're fucking him?"

For the love of God. "That is none of your business, but no, I'm not. I am focused on my children and my job."

"You mean job—"

"I am a great mom. Don't you dare discredit that. Wife, sure, I sucked, but you weren't good to me."

"Whatever. No, I won't give you a weekend, and you're lucky my lawyer doesn't think I have a case to get rid of that nanny. But if I hear he's done anything to my boys—"

"He'd never," I reiterate. "He's a good man."

"You heard me."

I close my eyes and hate how mad he makes me. I don't want to fight with him. All it does is make me hate him more, and I don't want that. I have to deal with him for the rest of my life because no matter what, he'll always be the boys' father. Damn it, why does he make this so hard? I don't want to do this, I don't, but damn it, I have to do something. I'll do anything for my boys.

"If I give you spring break, will you give me one weekend a month with the boys?"

He pauses, and my stomach churns. "I'd need that in writing."

"Which is fine, as long as I get in writing that we are changing the parenting plan, that I'd get them one weekend a month, and you'll get the other three."

"That would mean I wouldn't see them for one whole week a month. That's not okay with me."

I think that over, and I wipe my face. "How about on Tuesday, you pick them up from practice and keep them overnight. You usually don't travel until Wednesdays anyway. Lincoln can make sure they are packed and ready to go."

He clears his throat, and I can just see him sitting there thinking this over. I know he wants to say no just to stick it to me, but I know he wants spring break with the boys.

Ah, shit, the boys. "I'll need to talk to them about this."

"The boys?" Simon asks.

"Yes. I'll need to make sure they are okay with this change. I hate throwing so much change at them."

"I do too."

"Holy shit. Something we agree on." He chuckles, and I sort of smile, though I don't mean it. "I'd ask too that you let Lincoln be."

He hesitates. "I guess I can try."

"I appreciate that. He really is good for the boys."

"From what I'm told, they like him a lot."

"They do. I mean, no one has run into duct tape yet."

He laughs once more. "They get that wild side from you."

I smile. "Maybe."

I'm met with silence once more, and my stomach is in knots.

"So you'll talk to the boys and get back to me?"

"I will, and then we can get the lawyers on the paperwork."

"Sounds good to me."

I let out the breath I was holding, and my tears run faster down my face. "Thank you."

"Yeah. Talk to you later."

"Yeah," I say, hanging up, and when the phone hits the receiver, a sob leaves my lips. I may have just won what I wanted to win, but in a way, I feel like nothing but a loser. I never thought I'd have to bargain with who I assumed was the love of my life to get time with my kids.

And I still have eight years left doing just that with him.

Standing in front of my bathroom mirror, I dry my hair as my body tingles from the hot shower I just took. Richard found me crying in my office and sent me home. I hadn't meant for him to catch me, but after a long talk with my lawyer, who insisted I don't give up my spring break, I felt a little defeated. I know that's the only way Simon will give me the boys for a weekend, though. I really had no other choice; plus, I couldn't get off for spring break anyway. They'd sit at home with Lincoln, but still, I was bummed to say the least.

While I was thankful to be off early, I soon realized I wouldn't be home in time to take Charlie to therapy. Instead of sitting in the house feeling sorry for myself, I decided to take a shower and be ready for when they all got home. Hopefully I can persuade them to go to dinner with me, though I'm sure I won't have to do much convincing. They'll want to go. I just hope Lincoln hasn't started anything for dinner. When I got home, there was nothing cooking, so that made me excited for the possible dinner night with my boys.

And maybe Lincoln would want to go.

I'm not sure if that is a good idea, but I want his company. It was a tough day, and while I usually call Riana to talk it out, I want to talk to him. Get one of his quick smiles and feel better instantly. It is pathetic and childish since I want something I can't have, but I like him. He is fun, and I need fun after the day I had.

Looking at myself, though, I find I'm not satisfied with my appearance. My thick face and the wrinkles by my eyes—I don't know how Lincoln could ever see me as anything more than a mom. His boss. He is unbelievably beautiful, and I'm just average. I couldn't even keep my husband from cheating on me. I'm pathetic. Jesus, I'm riding that pity train like crazy right now.

Shaking my head, I move product through my hair, ignoring my woes. I won't let them get me down. I'm okay. The boys are doing better, and damn it, I am going to be great one day. Just have to get over the speed bumps. I reach for my hair dryer and turn it on just as my phone rings. I see it's Lincoln, and my pussy clenches.

I really need to get control of that.

But apparently I have no control over my body when it comes to my manny.

I turn the hair dryer off and answer, "Hello?"

"Hey, it's me."

"I know."

He laughs. "So therapy went well. He told me that they just talked about stupid stuff. I tried to get him to tell me what that meant, but he wouldn't elaborate."

I nod. "Probably about fixing his relationship with his dad."

"Which reminds me... I wanted to call you earlier, but I wasn't sure if I could."

"You can always call me," I insist as I sit on the edge of the tub. "What's up?"

"So this morning, he told me the reason he didn't want to go to school was because Simon was coming to have lunch with him. Apparently he wants Charlie to talk to you about letting the boys spend spring break with him."

"Ah," I say, closing my eyes. "Simon told me he was going to do that."

"I told him to talk to you."

"What did he say?"

"He said he would."

"Well, good. I have to talk to them. I think I'm going to do it."

"Really?"

"Yeah, I want to have a weekend with the boys each month, and that is the only thing that I could use to get it."

"I don't like that guy."

I laugh. "I don't either."

"But I guess it is a smart move."

"You think so?"

"I do," he says softly, his voice tickling my insides. "Yeah, you'll lose spring break with them, but the weekends will far surpass that time with them."

I smile. "That's what I was thinking."

"Cool. What?" he says, pausing, and I'm confused. "No. Did you leave it in the car?"

I hear one of the twins in the distance, and I smile. "They probably did."

But he doesn't hear me. "Let me call you back."

"Sure—"

But he hangs up before I can get the whole word out. I smile to myself as I set my phone down. I like that he has gotten Charlie to open up a little bit and that he is giving me a heads-up. I need it and pray they will go for what I proposed to Simon earlier.

I feel like a ball of nerves as I turn the hair dryer back on. I am tight everywhere, and I almost don't want to talk to the boys about it yet. I'm not sure I can do it without being emotional. I don't want to give up my week, but I want more time with them, and maybe, just maybe, this is a door that both Simon and I could go through to see we can compromise on stuff. But then, who am I kidding? That man is hell bent on ruining my life.

Groaning, I run my hand through my hair as I dry it as fast as I can. Even the music playing doesn't calm me, and that's unusual for me. I'm on edge. I don't even dance or sing. I just dry my hair, going over and over again in my head what I would say to the boys. I don't want to hurt them by changing more things, but maybe they'll be okay with it. Ugh. I don't know.

Once my hair is dry, I throw it up in a bun before taking my towel off and hanging it over the shower. Walking through my bathroom to my room, I sit on the edge of my bed and reach for my lotion. Running it down my arms, my shoulders. I rub it into my breasts, closing my eyes as I move my fingers along my nipples. What I need is a release, a good one that will shatter all these nerves out of my body.

What a wonderful idea.

Get my vibrator and think of that damn ducky towel Lincoln was wearing, and I'll get off in seconds.

I reach over to my nightstand and get my vibrator out. Lubing it up, I inhale deeply, lie back in my bed, and open my legs. I move my fingers along my pussy, parting my mouth as I open myself up. I find my clit before I turn it on, and when I do, the vibrating sound is soothing. I press it against my clit and cry out a bit as I jerk up, my body is so tight I know it won't take much. Running it down to my opening, I grab hold of my ankle as I fuck myself with my vibrator, my cries getting louder each time I work it in and out of my pussy.

I feel it building. My toes are curling, and my heart is pounding.

I know what I need.

I need him.

In that rubber ducky towel.

A smile comes over my lips as I move the vibrator faster inside me, seeing the length of him. He's so thick, mouthwatering, that all I want is him deep inside me. In my head, I've ripped the damn towel off, and his cock is deep inside me, doing what my vibrator is doing.

"Oh, oh, yes," I cry out as I move it faster. "Yes."

"Holy fuck."

I freeze.

No, that is in my head. All in my head.

But when I open my eyes, tilting my head back toward my door, I find that it isn't in my head.

Nope. It's Lincoln.

Standing in my doorway.

And just as the laundry basket he is holding hits the ground, I mutter, "Oh, fuck."

# CHAPTER THIRTEEN

## LINCOLN

I don't move.

I'm so fucking hard I'm pretty sure my cock will break if I do. I didn't even realize the laundry basket I was holding fell until her eyes come up from it to meet mine. Those eyes. They're huge and full of shock, though if I'm honest, that's not what I'm looking at.

I'm looking at the flush of her skin.

Her thick hips and breasts.

Her shaved cunt.

Seeing her sprawled out like that has me convinced I've never seen anything more magnificent. Pulling in a deep breath, I can only blink as she gets up quickly, the vibrator she is using hitting the ground with a *thunk*. Pulling the covers up, she covers her bits as best as she can as she gawks at me.

"What are you doing?"

I still can't speak, though. I'm completely speechless, and my body is shaking with want. I have to have her.

But I made a promise.

But she's gorgeous. I want her.

But she's my boss.

Fuck it, I am *desperate* for her.

Stepping over the laundry basket, I move toward her. She takes a step back, her eyes about popping out of her head, but I can't stop myself as I come toe to toe with her, my hands shaking at my sides. "Tell me no."

"Huh?" she gasps, her breathing so hard.

The damn buzzing from the vibrator is distracting as fuck, but it doesn't matter as I get lost in the lust swirling in her eyes. "Tell me no," I say once more, this time low and raspy. My cock is so damn hard, my balls tight, and I don't know what I'll do if she does say no. Her eyes burn into mine, and I can see when she realizes what I am saying.

What I am asking for.

Slowly, she shakes her head before whispering, "I can't."

I growl in response, pulling the blanket from her grip. She lets out a cry before I reach for the back of her head, crashing my mouth to hers. She comes willingly, eagerly, her body pressing into mine as I squeeze my eyes shut, relief flooding me as I drink from her sweet lips. They are more than I could ever dream of. More than I even deserve. Snaking my arm around her waist, I grab hold of her ass, molding it in my hand as our mouths move together in such a perfect but desperate way.

I almost come at the feel of her. How many times have I lain awake at night, wishing I could hold her? Her body is soft, perfect, and fucking hell, I never want to let her go. But she pulls away first, ripping at my shirt, the buttons popping off before the fabric slides down my arms. As she makes quick work of my jeans, she runs her tongue along my chest, around my nipples as I toe out of my shoes. I am shaking, literally shaking, so hard I'm surprised I am able to get naked at all. Her hands explore my back, my ass, and it feels so fucking right as her mouth meets mine again.

Our lips just go together, as silly as it sounds, and I don't want to stop kissing her. I don't, but damn it, I gotta have more. Taking her by the back of the thighs, I lift her up, and she cries out before wrapping her arms around my neck. "Are you crazy?"

"Yeah, yeah, I am," I say, laying her down on the bed and pressing my cock against her. "I'm fucking nuts for you."

Her eyes glaze over as I kiss down her jaw, her chin lifting, giving me access to her neck. I have wanted to do this for as long as I've known her, and the taste and smell of her doesn't disappoint. Taking her by the back of her knees, I press her back into the bed as I slide my cock up and down her slick center and look down at her. She's covered in gooseflesh and flushed beyond belief. The sight drives me wild. I don't know what I want. To take her pussy in my mouth or fuck until I can't take it.

Licking her lips, she moves her hands up and down my arms. "You look confused."

My lips tilt. "I don't know what I want. I want it all."

Her eyes shine. "All?"

"I want to eat you, fuck you, and then eat you some more. I'm struggling. Give me a second."

I'm answered with giggles as her hands come around my neck, bringing me down to her. Her lips move along mine as she whispers, "Maybe I want you so far down the back of my throat, I have that moment of fear that I won't be able to breathe."

I'm going to die.

Right there.

"Nope, can't handle that," I decide before her grin presses against my lips. I kiss her lips and push myself up from the bed before standing. "I'm going to fuck you. Right now, and I can't go easy."

"I don't want you to."

Yup. Dead.

Reaching down for my jeans, I grab a condom. I tear the package open and grip my cock as I slide the condom on, drinking in every single inch of her. "God, I've wanted you since the moment I met you."

Her eyes are hooded and her lips part as she moves her hands down her stomach. "You have?"

"Oh, fuck yes." I moan as I grab hold of one of her legs.

"I couldn't tell."

"Because you were fighting it," I say, taking hold of her other leg. She cries out as I guide myself into her and go to the hilt. "And I was too."

When I start to move out, ever so slowly, I'm met with the most amazing moan, one that hits me straight in the gut, and fucking fuck, that dude is an idiot for leaving her. For I'm pretty damn sure I just found my cock's home. Gripping her by the back of her thighs, I move in and out of her, each thrust harder and more demanding. Her body moves with each of my thrusts, her breasts bouncing as she digs her nails into my arms. Her eyes are closed, her back arching as I pound into her, needing all of her. Every single ounce.

Wrapping her legs around me, she grips hard as her

orgasm hits. I wasn't even ready, it is so fast, and when she cries out, I am in awe of her beauty. Taking me by my arms, she brings me down and kisses me as her pussy clenches my cock. Nibbling at my bottom lip, she smiles at me before whispering, "Your turn."

I'm confused until she rolls us over, getting on top of me before she starts to move up and down my cock. Taking hold of her ass, I guide her as my toes curl, and I memorize every single inch of her body. She is perfect. Fucking perfect. Pressing her hands to my chest, she moves her legs up over my thighs, cupping my balls with her feet as she bounces on my cock. I've never had a woman ride me like this or look as fucking great as Vera does. Breathless, I hold on to her hips as she goes deeper and deeper, my cock so deep inside her I honestly can't take it.

I try to hold off, but I've been thinking of this woman for way too long to even try. Squeezing her hip, I yell out as my knees come up, stopping her but also pushing her forward so she comes down, her mouth a breath from mine. A grin is on her face as she moves her fingers along my jaw until they are lost in the hair on my chin. She runs her tongue along my lips, and I'm still jerking up into her, riding my orgasm as my mind catches up with my body.

What the hell did I just do?

And shit, why do I want way more?

Phillip is going to kill me.

But I don't care at the moment—not when her lips are moving with mine as I roll her to her side, holding her tightly to me. How can I worry about that? I have the woman I have been wanting in my arms, and yes, things are about to get very complicated, but I don't have to worry about that yet. All I have to worry about is making her come over and over again.

Well, until I have to go get the boys.

Her eyes burn into mine as she moves her nose against my nose. "Gah. Thank you."

I open my eyes, confused. "Thank you?"

She grins at me. "Lord knows I needed that."

Oh.

Moving my hand up her hip, I squeeze it. "Did you want it?"

"Oh, yes, so bad."

Oh, there is still hope.

"But you were right. I'm glad I didn't waste a fuck on someone who didn't matter."

Nope. There went the hope out the window.

As she kisses my nose, she rolls out of the bed and reaches down. When she sits up, she has her vibrator in her hand; it's still going like crazy. "This thing is loud," she says with a giggle, but I'm still flabbergasted.

Because I'm pretty sure I was just used.

# CHAPTER FOURTEEN

## VERA

"Oh no. What did that asshole Simon do now?"

Taking in a shaky breath, I shake my head quickly, though Riana can't see me. No one can. I'm hiding in my bathroom after Lincoln just left to get the boys from practice. I couldn't face him. Oh, my God, I'm disgusting. "No, it's not him."

I can't believe what I said. I can't believe that I'm basically hiding in the bathroom and not coming out. I'm just so damn embarrassed.

"What? Then why are you calling me crying? Do I need to come over?"

"No," I cry, dropping my face into my hands. I want to curl into a ball and melt into the floor. I know it's impossible, but damn it, I wish I could. "I think I messed everything up with Lincoln."

Riana goes silent. "Shit, V. What did you do?"

My lip wobbles. "I slept with him."

She takes in a quick breath. "No way."

My eyes fall shut, the embarrassment rushing over me. "I did, and oh, my God, Riana, it was perfect, honestly. I've never felt so alive in my life, but when we were done, he's looking in my eyes, ready for round two, and all these emotions hit me like crazy. I thought I just wanted to fuck someone, but I could honestly go at it with him over and over again and be okay with that." I groan, my body still vibrating from his touch. "Actually, more than okay."

"I don't understand what's wrong, then..."

"I can't lose him as a nanny, Riana. He is amazing, and I finally got Simon to accept him, and I thought I was just crushing on him, but damn it, I felt something in his arms that I haven't felt in a really long time."

Her voice is full of such concern, and all it does is rattle my soul even more. I can't believe I just fucked this up. "For fuck's sake, V. What the hell did you do?"

I cover my face once more, groaning as my tears run down my face. "I freaked and said I was glad I didn't waste a fuck on just anyone." She groans, and more tears roll down my face. "I know."

"Why would you say that?"

"'Cause that's what it needs to be—a fuck—and I was ready to accept that, but Riana, his eyes said so much more, and when I said what I did, he looked as if I'd slapped him."

"Oh, Vera. Why..." she groans.

I shake my head, squeezing my eyes shut. "I don't know. I'm an idiot."

"You are."

"But I was so worried that he'd be the one to say it and break my heart."

"So you say it? Jesus, couldn't just wait it out?"

"I'm an idiot, remember?"

"Damn it. Where is he?"

"He went to get the boys."

"What did he say when he left?"

"We really didn't say anything after I dropped that bomb. I got up and went to the bathroom, and then after a bit, he came to the door and said he was gonna get the kids."

"Ugh, Vera."

"I know."

"You gotta talk to him."

I shake my head. "I don't even think I can ever face him."

"You have to."

"Then what do I say?"

"I don't know, but you better figure it out!"

Closing my eyes, I wish I saw the rubber duckies and not his eyes that were swirling with rejection. I'm not the type to make people feel like that. I'm not fucking Simon! I just freaked. My insecurities came out of nowhere, not believing that he'd want me again. I still can't believe he took me the way he did, with such determination. Such need. I was on a high, but when he looked at me, I freaked. What if it was just the heat of the moment? What if he is the one using me? But I know none of that is true. I was such a jerk.

I'm sure Riana agrees.

Her voice is strained as she says, "When I said to sleep with him, I meant it because I knew that you guys would be good together. I never thought you'd tell him he is just a fuck! He must feel so used."

I groan loudly. "I know. I'm an awful person. I don't want him to feel like that."

"You're not an awful person, but don't try to make excuses. You're scared, for good reasons, but crap, V, think before you speak!"

"I'm out of practice—"

"Come on, Vera. If you don't want to be this person you're acting like, then fix it, because if you don't, you're for sure ruining things with him."

"I know." She is absolutely right, and I don't want that. I like Lincoln a lot, and that scares me. He made love to me. He didn't just fuck me, and I think that's what scared the hell out of me. I haven't been done like that in years, but what the hell am I supposed to do? Apologize, and then what? I don't know.

Damn it.

♦ ♦ ♦ ♦

I'm waiting in the kitchen when the boys and Lincoln walk in. When the twins see me, their faces break into grins. "Mom!"

My heart fills with joy as they come to me, wrapping their arms around me. Even Charlie is smiling. "I thought you were working late."

I hug the boys tightly. "Well, good news, I moved my schedule around, and now I'll be home early on Thursdays and Fridays to be with you guys!"

"Really!" Louis gushes, as Elliot asks, "Promise?"

"Yup! And to celebrate, I wanted to take you guys to dinner. How does that sound?"

"Awesome!" they both cheer.

"Well, where are we going?" Charlie asks.

I glance over at him. "You guys choose."

"Pizza!" they all agree in unison before running up the stairs to shower and dress.

And to think, I didn't even have to coax them.

But with them rushing up the stairs, it leaves Lincoln and me alone.

I look up at him, my face flushing red as I clear my throat, but before I can even try to say something, he goes, "I'm going to head out. I'll see you in the morning."

He won't even look at me, but I have to stop him. "Actually, I was going to ask you to join us. My treat."

He shakes his head before turning most of his body to the door. He wants to leave; his body is basically screaming that. "I'm going to pass. I got stuff to do tonight."

"Oh."

"Yeah," he says simply, tucking his hands in his pockets. "So I'll—"

"Can you cancel them? Figured it would be fun to celebrate, and I wanted to talk to you."

He shakes his head. "No, I can't."

"You can't, or you don't want to?"

He looks back at me then, and I swear the hurt is swirling in the depths of his gray eyes. "I don't want to."

That hurts more than it should.

Biting into my lip, I ask, "Can we talk now, then?"

"About what?" he asks, his eyes holding mine.

"About what happened earlier."

He shakes his head. "Why?"

"Because I feel we left a lot unsaid."

"There is nothing to talk about," he answers, and I can see

that there is; he just doesn't want to talk about it. "Usually when you—" He pauses, looking up the stairs before glancing back at me. His voice is low as he says, "When you fuck, it's usually a one-time thing unless both parties want to do it again, and I don't think that's a good idea. Do you?"

"I don't know," I say, and he gawks at me, almost like he's disgusted with me. Looking down, I swallow past the lump in my throat. "I feel we need to talk about it still."

"Why? It's over. I'm going to do my job, and that's that. Got it out of our systems, I guess."

"No, that's—"

But before I can finish, Elliot is running down the stairs, coming to a halt in front of Lincoln. "Linc, are you going to come?"

He shakes his head. "Sorry, bud, I have things to do tonight, and plus, you can spend time with your mom! I know you've missed her."

Elliot's smile grows as he nods. "Yeah, true, but I want you there."

Lincoln wraps an arm around his neck. "I'll see you in the morning. Tell your brothers bye for me."

"Okay." He laughs when Lincoln starts to give him a noogie. "Bye."

But as Lincoln walks off, he doesn't spare me another look like he usually does.

Or say goodbye.

Yup, I fucked up big-time.

# CHAPTER FIFTEEN

## LINCOLN

"So Mom is going to get a weekend with us now, Linc!"

I look in the rearview mirror at Elliot and nod. "Is that right?"

"Yup," Louis says with a grin on his little face. "And we get to go to Universal."

"Wow! With your dad and Kaia?"

"Yup," they both say.

I don't miss the way Charlie mumbles something. "Are you not excited?"

"I want my mom to go," he says simply, looking at me. "She said that she'll take us later, but I know she wants to go."

"But she promised, Charlie," Elliot says. "She said she isn't mad."

"Yeah, but—"

"She isn't," I interject. I could hear the dismay in Elliot's voice. "She told me that she wants you guys to go since she'd have to work anyway."

Charlie looks down at his phone as he mutters, "But she had to give it up to have a weekend with us."

"And that is her choice."

"What is?" Elliot asks, and I shake my head as I pull into the driveway.

"Nothing, bud. It's all good. I'm excited for you guys."

He beams as Louis bounces in his seat, but then he stops suddenly. "Sucks, though. Mom will be bored while we're gone."

"Yeah," Elliot says sadly as I turn off the car.

Everyone files out as Charlie says, "She'll probably just work the whole time."

"But when she gets home, she'll be lonely," Louis explains as we walk up the walkway.

"I'm sure she'll find something to do," Charlie decides, but then I notice that Elliot is staring at me.

"What's up?"

"You should come hang with Mom while we're gone," he says simply. "You can cook her dinner."

Louis bounces beside me. "I have fifty dollars! I can pay you."

I smile as I wrap my arm around his neck. "You're a good kid, Louis."

"I have a hundred," Charlie says then, and I glance back at him as he shuts the door, a bit surprised. "She'll be hungry, and she probably won't clean 'cause she's busy."

Vera has no clue how lucky she is. "Keep your money, guys. Buy me something nice in Universal. You know I love me some Simpsons." All three laugh, even Charlie, and I grin back at them as I nod. "But I'll talk to her and see if she wants me to come over."

"Thanks," the twins gush as they start up the stairs.

"Start packing for your dad's."

"Okay," they agree as they run up the stairs, but then I notice Charlie is not running with them.

"Are you not going up?"

"I wanted to ask you something."

"Sure," I say, leaning against the back of the couch. "You okay?"

He nods but then toes the hardwood. "There is this girl at school—"

I probably shouldn't have smiled as wide as I did, but I couldn't help it. But when he starts to walk away, mumbling something along the lines of "Forget it," I stop him, laughing as I pull him back to me.

"There is a girl?"

He looks nervous as he tucks his hands into his pockets. "She's really pretty, and I want to ask for her number. How do I do that?"

My heart almost can't take it. Within seconds, I'm back to the moment when the oldest Ellenton kid, Matthew, asked me the same thing. But this isn't Matthew. It's Charlie. Sitting back against the couch, I clap my hands together. "Do you guys have class together?"

"We do."

"Can you pass her a note?"

He shakes his head. "No, I want to do it face-to-face so if she turns me down, at least it's to my face and not with her stupid friends or something."

I laugh. "Smart man. Okay, so walk up to her locker and smile." He eyes me, but I keep smiling. He waits, but I'm still smiling very obnoxiously at him.

"Why are you smiling at me like that?"

"I want you to smile."

He groans loudly and gives me a fake smile.

"That will not get you a number."

He scoffs, but thankfully I'm rewarded with a smile that mirrors Vera's.

It takes my breath away, but I ignore my heart and say, "There you go. Now go to her, smile like that, and tell her that you like whatever you like about her, and when she smiles back, ask for her number."

"Just like that?"

"Just like that."

"And it will work?"

"It will."

"Cool, thanks."

"You're welcome," I say as he heads up the stairs, taking them two at a time. Sitting there, I can't help but think about Vera. I hope like hell it goes different for my main man than it has for me, but I sure do like when I'm rewarded with Vera's smile.

A lot.

Letting out a long sigh, I glance at the clock, surprised Vera isn't home yet. I could text her, but I don't want to. I'll just wait. But by the time Vera walks in, it is with Simon, and I'm annoyed.

"I'm so sorry I'm late, guys," she complains as she comes to each boy, hugging them tightly. "There was a wreck in the city, and I couldn't get to the train. When I did, there was maintenance. I'm really sorry."

"There was maintenance when I went through earlier today too," Simon says then, gathering the boys' bags. When he looks over at me, I stand up a little taller. I know he doesn't like me. "Hey there, Lincoln."

I nod. "Hey."

He makes a face before going to the door. "You guys ready?"

I can tell they aren't, but Vera can handle that. This is my cue to leave. "I'm gonna go."

Vera holds out her hand, stopping me. "No, can you wait? I have payment for you."

*Fuck.*

"Yeah," I say simply as she continues to say goodbye to the boys. She doesn't want to let them go, and I don't think they want to leave either. I hate that she isn't home in time to spend more time with them, but I'm pretty sure I don't hate is as much as she does. I can see it all in her eyes.

With one more hug, they start out the door, and I notice Simon hands Vera an envelope.

"Thank you."

"Yeah. I'll see you Sunday."

"Have a nice weekend, guys."

As she shuts the door, she looks back to me. "Let's go to the kitchen."

"Don't you have the check?"

"No, I haven't filled it out."

Ugh. I really want to go. Walking behind her, I try so damn hard not to look at her ass, but I fail miserably. There is something about this woman's backside in a dress that gives me the ultimate hard-on. As she goes around the island, she takes out her purse, stuffing the envelope in it before she reaches inside. I assume she is getting a check, and when she does, I see there is something bright green stuck to it. She sets it down on the counter and slides it to me. I'm confused.

Reaching for it, I see that it's a green sticky note on an already filled-out check.

*I'm sorry.*

I look up at her as I rip off the note and crumple it up. "Nothing to be sorry for."

"Actually, there is."

"What?"

"I should have never said what I did, because I don't feel that way at all," she says quickly, her eyes never leaving mine. "I have lusted for you since I met you, and when I got what I had been literally dreaming about for the last couple of weeks, I panicked."

*Keep yourself in check, Scott. This means nothing.*

"Panicked?"

She looks down, moving her fingers together. "I felt all sorts of things, and I wasn't sure I was supposed to."

Leaning on the island, I capture her gaze when she looks at me. "Like what?"

Her face changes, her cheeks getting redder by the second. "Like I didn't want it to end and I didn't want you to leave my bed. How I still want you more than my next breath and that

I was nowhere near done exploring you. I hadn't even gotten to taste you, deep down my throat, and I wasn't sure how to handle that. I wanted you so damn bad, and I just freaked."

Everything went red hot. I couldn't control my body if I wanted. "Is that right?"

"Yeah."

With a nod, I set the check on the table and then hop up on the island.

Her eyes widen. "What are you doing?"

Stepping off, I drop to my feet right in front of her, her gaze meeting mine as she takes in a harsh breath. "Walking around is too far. I wanted to be right here, right now."

Her voice is breathy as she whispers, "Lincoln—"

"And how about now?" I ask, cutting her off. "How do you feel now?"

Her lips press together. They're so luscious, and all I want is to kiss them while I get lost in her brown gaze. But I have to know. Still in a whisper, she says, "I can't stop thinking about you even when I try so hard. All I do is think of you, and I want you."

I grab the back of her neck and pull her to me, taking her mouth with mine.

Because that is all I needed to hear.

# CHAPTER SIXTEEN

## VERA

Oh...oh, sweet Lord.

I press myself against Lincoln's hard body and our arms tangle as we grasp for each other, needing each other, before I can wrap them around his neck. Our mouths move just as perfectly as they did the day before. I have never been kissed by someone like this. His kisses are demanding and rough; they're honestly mind-blowing. I thread my fingers in his hair, and he runs his tongue with mine and slides his hands down my body. He takes the fabric of my dress in his hand, balling it up as he tries to pull me closer.

He wants me.

Just as bad as I want him.

When he squeezes his arms around my waist, my dress goes up farther and my ass peeks out, but I don't care. I don't care about anything but kissing this man. Tearing his mouth from mine, he brings his gaze to mine, and again I see that look. I don't know what the look is since I've never experienced it a day in my life, but it gives me crazy butterflies in my gut.

Butterflies, at thirty-one...

*Wow.*

His eyes are hooded, and such lust swirls in them as he moves his nose with mine, both of us catching our breath. Balling my dress up, he pulls it higher, his eyes never leaving mine as he grabs hold of my ass cheek. "Do you know how wild this ass makes me?"

My lips quirk. "Seriously?"

"Yes," he practically groans, molding it in his palm. "I swear I stare at it every chance I get."

I'm fully smiling by now, lost in his gaze. "I will never look at rubber duckies the same."

His face breaks into a grin before he takes my mouth with his once more. My eyes fall shut as I feel him grow against me. He's so long and thick, and my mouth is watering to get him between my lips. Sloppily, he kisses down my cheek, my jaw, before sucking and nibbling on my neck. His lips are torture, but his teeth are downright dangerous. I lengthen my neck for him, and he licks as he runs his teeth along my neck, squeezing my hips in his large hands. When he turns me in his arms, pressing his hands into my stomach, I gasp, letting my head fall back against his shoulder as our mouths meet once more. Teasing, demanding kisses that curl my toes in my pumps.

Sliding his hand down my stomach, he gathers my dress before pulling it up over my hips and taking my pussy with his other hand. Still his mouth moves on mine, my moans becoming more demanding as he draws circles around my wanton lips. "I haven't been able to stop thinking about your cunt," he whispers, running his lips along my jaw. "It's almost as gorgeous as you are."

Breathless, I lean into him. "I want your mouth on it."

"Oh, baby, that is a given, but I want to play."

"I can't," I groan, arching into his hand. "I want you now."

His chuckles against my neck. "I want to take my sweet time with you."

I groan loudly as he cups me, squeezing me softly as his other hand makes quick work of the buttons of my dress. Soon my bra is showing before he's pulling it down off my shoulders, his lips replacing where the fabric was as I kick off my shoes. I pull at my dress before it falls to my feet. After yanking the cups down on my bra, he molds my breast and then kisses and licks my shoulders and neck. "So fucking gorgeous," he mutters against my skin, and I can't breathe.

I've never been worshiped before, and I was married for ten years, but I feel like that is exactly what Lincoln is doing.

He unclasps my bra, and I close my eyes, desire shaking my core. He kisses down my back, and my head falls back as a whimper leaves my lips.

"Ah, this ass," he says so rough, it makes me smile. Molding my ass, he kisses each cheek before running his mouth along them. "Do you always wear thongs?"

I giggle. "I do."

"Ugh. I think I just came," he says, and I laugh louder.

"Well, recharge. We have a lot to do."

Nipping at my ass, he makes me jump. "You got that right."

He then turns me around, and my ass hits against the island as he trails kisses down my belly. I want to be self-conscious, I do, but I don't feel that way under his gaze.

I feel beautiful, wanted.

As he pushes my thong down my legs, he kisses my thighs,

running his tongue along the inside of them before taking my ass in his hands once more. When he glances up at me, I'm holding my breath.

God, he looks good down there.

His eyes are so bright, his lips swollen from our kisses, and I swear the freckles along his nose make me swoon. His hair is a mess, but damn it, I've never seen anyone so gorgeous. And I quiver from his touch when he kisses my lips, his eyes never leaving mine. Breathless, I hold the island as he moves his tongue along my lips. When he opens me up, his gaze cuts to my pussy, but it's only for a second before his gaze is back on mine, and he's found my clit. Coming off the island, I arch into his mouth as he devours me wholly. His fingers bite into my ass as he's sucking me, and I swear my whole body is shaking against him.

Letting my head fall back, I squeeze the edge of the island as his name falls from my lips, my knuckles for sure going white. Suddenly, he lifts my legs over his shoulders and raises me up, pushing me back on the island. My head hits the sprayer on the sink, but I'm so lost in my passion I don't care at all. I just slide along as he continues to suck me into oblivion.

When he presses his thumb to my opening, I cry out, feeling my orgasm coming. My legs are shaking, my body is burning, and when he slides two of his fingers inside me, his tongue flicking against my clit, I'm lost. He has the perfect rhythm, and I feel everything go tight before I explode.

Arching off the island, I cry out as I jerk against his mouth. When he takes me by the hips, holding me down as he continues to suck me, my cries get louder, his name falling off my lips as I try to get away, but he doesn't let me. He slides his tongue down my slit and then fucks me with it, and I can't fight him.

I feel like Jell-O.

"Fuck, you taste good."

I can't even comment. My heart is pounding, my body is shaking, and everything is a little blurry. "I think I came too hard."

I'm met with his laughter as I hear the tear of a condom. "I'm not done yet."

Breathless, I tease, "I was worried about that."

I whimper as I open my eyes. He's naked, beautiful and stunningly naked.

Good Lord. It's like seeing him for the first time.

Again his chuckles run down my spine before he takes me by my ankles, pulling me down the island to him. He enters me with a demanding thrust, and I squeeze him as I cry out, my fingers biting into his biceps. He's so fucking big, but he fits me, and boy, does it feel fucking good. I meet his gaze as he pulls out of me ever so slowly before thrusting hard back inside me. His eyes are hooded, and sweat has gathered around his forehead. His eyes are like storm clouds, the kind that always come before a really bad tornado would hit back home.

"Beautiful."

His lips quirk. "That's what I was going to say."

My face breaks into a grin as he takes me by the arms, pulling me up before wrapping them around his neck. "Hold on."

I do as he says before he lifts me. As my legs come around

his waist, he turns us, slamming me into the fridge before thrusting up into me, so hard it takes my breath away.

But I fucking love it.

Magnets hit the ground, papers of the twins' artwork go flying as Lincoln pounds up into me, his fingers for sure leaving marks on my ass from where he is holding on to me so tightly. I swear I feel each thrust in my chest, and soon my orgasm is building once more.

"Kiss me."

My eyes widen as I meet his hooded gaze. "Huh?"

"Kiss me. I want your mouth, now," he demands, but then, before I can even agree or kiss him, he captures my mouth with such need. Soon, his kisses become harder. Each one taking my breath away as my orgasm keeps building. He's hitting all the right spots, and I swear I'm going to applaud him later for holding my ass up and fucking me like this.

Because I feel incredible.

And he looks incredible.

His shoulders are covered with a sheen of sweat, his back feels amazing under my fingers, but it's his mouth that tips me over the edge. It hits me like a ton of bricks, and I'm clinging to him as a roaring moan leaves my lips. His face presses into my neck as he continues to thrust up inside me. Each one harder and deeper, and I swear I seriously can only hold on as he takes what he wants.

Which I assume is everything.

When his mouth comes crashing against mine, I raise my hands to cup his face as he jerks up inside me and then stills. His legs are shaking and so are mine as he pulls away, only a breath before moving his nose with mine. Kissing my top lip, he squeezes my waist before lowering us down to the floor. The cool hardwood is welcoming against my hot skin, but he doesn't allow me to touch it much as he pulls me close to him, holding me tightly. When he trails kisses along my top lip, I smile. "I'm glad someone has cleaned the floors."

He scoffs, kissing my bottom lip. "Me too, because I can't move."

"Me either."

He opens his eyes; they're so light, so beautiful, and I swear that look is back. The one that gives me the chills. Blinking, unsure of all the feelings that are assaulting me left and right, I hold his gaze.

"You're stunning, Vera. Honestly."

He inhales hard, letting it out just as hard, but I can't breathe.

For as I watch him, I know I am in so much fucking trouble.

# CHAPTER SEVENTEEN

## LINCOLN

Moving my hand down Vera's back to her backside and then back up, I close my eyes as I welcome the coolness of the floor. Turning my head, I nuzzle my nose in her hair as she pops a strawberry into her mouth. A smile curves when she holds one up to me. Taking it between my lips, I whisper, "Thanks."

"You're the one who got them for me, so it's only right I feed you."

I kiss her temple, inhaling hard, and I feel so incredibly spent. My whole body hasn't stopped tingling since the moment I touched her. I want her again, so much, but I'm unable to move at the moment. I have to say, holding her like this, feeling her body move with each inhale, maybe is just as good as being deep inside her.

Maybe.

Let's not get crazy here.

She is a minx. That's all there is to it. The sounds she made still have my heart racing in my chest. The way she kisses, the way her thighs wrap around my waist, the way she tastes... I honestly have no clue how Simon ever cheated on her or left her. For me, she's everything I've ever wanted and more. I don't know how I waited as long as I did.

His loss is my gain, I guess.

When she turns to me, her eyes dark and hooded, she holds another strawberry to my lips. I smile as I take a bite. Her hair is a tousled mess, and her body is still covered in such a beautiful flush. Her lipstick is smeared, and little curls have gathered around her forehead from sweat. I find her magnificent.

"You're beautiful."

Her face warms. "Stop," she groans as she hides her face in my beard. "You're making me all shy and shit."

I gather her closer in my arms. "That's what I want."

"Well, you're succeeding."

"Good," I mutter, kissing along her temple. "Don't act like you don't know how gorgeous you are."

She scoffs. "I don't."

I roll my eyes. "I won't even dignify that claim. It's blasphemy."

She snorts. "You're insane."

"No, you are, because whenever I look at you, I'm stunned by your beauty."

I can feel her smiling as she moves her fingers through the patch of hair on my chest.

"I guess when your husband cheats on you left and right, you don't feel as beautiful as you should."

I take hold of her ass and squeeze it. "Hey, don't let his issues take anything away from you. Especially now. You're good now."

She scoffs. "I don't feel good. Well, I mean I feel great

right now, but...I just feel a little lost."

"Why?"

"I don't know. There has been so much change for the boys the last couple of months. I feel like I'm constantly trying to balance everything in the most perfect way, but I can't figure it out. I either let my job down, or I let the boys down. I made myself sick with worry talking to them about getting a weekend with them, and they were so excited." She exhales hard, shaking her head. "I'm so hard on myself, and I want to be perfect because I apparently sucked as a wife, and it just rattles me." Her gaze meets mine. "Sorry, I'm venting."

"No, that's what I'm here for," I insist, kissing her cheek. "And I hear everything you're saying, but I really don't think you failed as a wife."

She gives me a deadpan look. "Then why did he cheat on me seven times?"

She laughs, but I don't hear a lick of humor in it, and my heart aches for her.

"I still wonder about that," she continues. "Isn't that pathetic? Like, why wasn't I good enough? I used to think it was because I gained so much weight with the twins, but that's not it because he cheated on me before that."

"I'm sorry... Seven times?" I ask, a little shocked. "I thought it was once."

She shakes her head and sits up. I want to take in her beautiful body, but her eyes are so sad as she moves her fingers together. "He cheated on me right after we found out I was pregnant with Charlie." She bites her lip. "I should have cut him out of my life then, but then I lost my parents, and he was all I knew. I mean, we'd dated since we were thirteen. He was the love of my life. So I stayed in touch, mostly for Charlie, but then we got back together when he came up here. Things were great, or so I thought. He was sleeping with his assistant, and I never knew."

"He's a jackass."

"That he is," she says sadly. "When I got pregnant with the twins, he promised me the world, and I believed him like a dumbass. I married him, and for once, I had the family I'd been yearning for since I lost my parents. We had it all, and I thought we were happy."

I reach out, taking her hand in mine. "He didn't deserve you."

She shrugs. "But even so, I never left. I was too comfortable, and I wanted so desperately for the boys to have both their parents since I didn't even have one. I couldn't bear to put them through a divorce, but Simon didn't care. When I found him in bed with Kaia, I didn't even cry. I just stood there, my heart dropping, because I knew we were done. He was always discreet, though I still found out, but this time, it was blatant. He wanted me to find him, and the fact that he did it with our boys downstairs, I couldn't accept that." My heart is in my gut as she rolls her eyes. "But then it didn't matter because he had already drawn up papers for divorce."

"I'm so sorry, Vera."

She shrugs. "What doesn't kill you makes you stronger is my motto."

I kiss her palm. "You deserve better than that."

"I finally realized that, that day, which is sad, since

yesterday is the first time I've had sex in six years."

My jaw drops. "No."

"Yeah, I mean, he didn't want me."

When her lips start to wobble, I reach for her, pulling her into my chest. "Well, he's a dumbass, because I can't think straight around you. I want you, Vera."

She kisses the middle of my chest, and I hold her tightly, wishing like hell I could explain how bad I want her. That I want her more than my next breath. That I never want to leave her. That I would treat her better than anyone in this world.

Especially that fuck Simon.

"Thank you."

I smile against her hair. "Stop thanking me. It's annoying."

She bites my chest. "It's polite."

"It's unnecessary. Everything I say is true. Also, don't ever feel like you're failing those boys. They inherited all your good traits."

Her eyes sparkle. "Why do you say that?"

"They offered me money to take care of you while they're in Orlando with Simon." Her lips curve, and when her eyes start to water up, I smile. "Don't you dare cry."

She laughs. "Did they?"

"Yes."

"What did you say?"

"I told them if you want me, then I'll be there."

She inhales hard, filling her lungs before letting it out in a whoosh. Pulling back, she reaches up before taking my jaw in her hand and moving her fingers through my beard. "Really?"

"Really," I promise, and I don't think she realizes how

deep that promise runs.

"You're a great man, Lincoln. Honestly."

I smile, wrapping an arm around her neck and pulling her closer to me. "And you're an amazing woman, Vera. Honestly. You need to realize that. No one can do what you do. You blow me away."

Her eyes sparkle before she crashes her mouth to mine in a heated embrace. Drawing the kiss out of me, she moves her hands down my neck, to my chest as I bring her into my lap, needing her closer. She straddles me, and my arms wrap around her waist as my cock meets her wonderfully wet center. Tearing her mouth from mine, she runs her tongue along my jaw, my neck, before sliding out of my lap onto her knees between my legs. Her ass is perfectly in the air as she goes on her hands, kissing down my stomach and dipping her tongue into my belly button. I take in a quick breath as she kisses down my thighs before grabbing my cock in her hand.

I jerk against her hand, a small moan leaving my lips as I watch her move her hand up and down my shaft. With her ass still in the air, her gaze meets mine as she runs her tongue along her lips. Shaking my head, I sigh deeply as I roughly say, "I can't with you."

Her lips curve. "I haven't even started."

"And I'm ready to blow."

I wish I could take a picture. I don't ever want to forget this image.

Her eyes deepen in color as she runs her tongue along the top of my cock. So slow it's torture as she continues to move her hand up and down me. She teases me, making me crazy as her tongue swirls around the tip. When her eyes meet mine, though, her hand stills before she takes me slowly, and as I disappear into her mouth, I swear I'm falling hard for this woman.

Hard.

The question is, is she falling for me?

Or has she been hurt so badly that I don't even have a chance?

# CHAPTER EIGHTEEN

## VERA

I don't think I can remember the last time I woke up with a man between my legs.

Come to think of it, I don't think I ever have.

When we were younger, Simon and I didn't wake up together. We had sex in the back of his truck or somewhere quick. Even when we were married, he wasn't the kind to roll over and have to have me.

But apparently, Lincoln is.

Moving his tongue down my chest, he grips my hips as he trails kisses between his licks. I crashed last night from exhaustion and was slightly surprised he had stayed. When I woke with him between my legs, looking like a Greek god, I was completely flabbergasted. I mean, don't get me wrong, I am really excited about it, but I almost think I dreamed the whole thing.

Because there is no way this is my reality.

But as Lincoln's fingers dig into my hips, his lips hovering over my aching center, there is no denying this.

He is here.

With me.

And boy, does he want me.

Closing my eyes, I widen my legs as he trails kisses down my thighs before running the tip of his tongue ever so slowly up my slit. A soft moan leaves my lips as he pushes my legs up and out so I'm completely open to him. Sliding his hands up under my ass, he holds me as he runs his nose along my wet lips, my whole body shaking in anticipation. His back flexes with each moment, and his shoulders are drool-worthy.

I almost don't understand how he is here with me, wanting me the way he does. But then his eyes cut to mine, and I swear, I've never felt so damn beautiful. I know that is pathetic and also a little unbelievable, but honestly, it's true. Even when Simon would say I looked good, I never believed him. His eyes always told a different story, but with Lincoln, there is no denying it because his eyes promise it. His body screams it, and his kisses make me feel it deep in my soul. It's such a weird feeling. Something so new, and if I'm honest, I like the way it makes me feel. A lot.

But right now, all I can think about is his tongue deep inside me.

Eagerly he licks me, sucking each lip into his mouth and biting softly before running his tongue up the center of me. When he squeezes my ass, my crack strains from his pull, but it feels damn good. His obsession with my ass only makes me wetter. I always thought it was massive, but he doesn't see it that way, and of course, that makes me feel a certain kind of way.

A scary way.

Closing my eyes, I arch against his mouth as he sucks my

clit into his lips, biting down softly. I'm lost in my pleasure, my moans coming out harsh and loud. Or at least I thought I was. He moves his hands from my ass, opening me up with one hand, and I gasp out when he presses his tongue to my clit. Then when he slides two fingers inside me, I'm crying out so loud, I'm sure the neighbors can hear me.

"Fucking hell, you're hot."

I'm thinking the same about him, but I can't even speak. Taking the sheets in my hands, I squeeze them tightly as I cry out, my heart pounding so damn hard in my chest. He fucks me quickly with his fingers, and his tongue does just as quick work. My body tightens, my toes curl, and I feel like everything just explodes inside me.

"Oh, Lincoln," I cry out, so loud it echoes in my room.

And all he does is chuckle.

Gasping for breath as he moves between my legs, I look up at the ceiling, but all I see is spots. When I move my legs apart even more, he lowers himself on top of me and thrusts inside me. My legs wrap around his waist as he presses his mouth to mine softly. Drawing the kisses out, he pushes deeper, if possible, and everything inside me clenches up once more. He's so big, fills me completely as his lips devour mine. Running my nails along his back, I tilt my hips, wanting him even deeper. Tearing his mouth from mine, he groans, his eyes squeezing shut as he keeps thrusting up inside me.

God, he is glorious.

Moving my hands up his back, I take him by the neck, threading my fingers into his hair. Capturing my mouth once more, he sweeps his tongue along mine, causing me to squeeze him with my thighs. Grinning against my lips, he kisses my bottom lip before pushing himself up and taking me by the back of the thigh. He looks down at me, and a smile pulls at my lips as he slowly moves out of me. His eyes are dark, swirling with desire, as he thrusts into me, hard, his arms straining as he grips my thighs. I'm in awe of him.

Moving my hands down his body, I take him by his wrist as he starts to speed up. Each thrust takes my breath away, and I feel it everywhere. Soon I feel myself building toward another release. Pushing my legs back farther, I watch as he watches himself disappear inside me. It's such a sight to see. When he pounds into me, our bodies slapping together, I let go. My release shakes my whole body as he slams into me, and I'm lost. His grip on my thighs is hard—I'm sure there will be a bruise later—but I can't feel anything. When he lets out a yell of his own, jerking inside me, I arch up as I squeeze his wrist, his name falling off my lips once more.

Lincoln stills as I take in a lungful of air. I'm shaking everywhere, my heart is pounding in my chest, and I swear I couldn't move even if I wanted to try. My legs are burning, my pussy is achy, but that's okay. Because when he lowers himself on top of me, taking my mouth with his once more, I feel utterly free.

And I'm not sure what that means.

◆ ◆ ◆ ◆

"I'm still convinced the neighbors probably know you stayed the night."

Lincoln looks over at me in the passenger seat, a little grin pulling at his lips. His eyes are playful as he squeezes my hand.

Yes. We are holding hands.

Like people who date.

I think we're dating.

"So? You're an adult."

"Yes, I am," I say dryly. "But I'm also newly divorced."

He makes a face. "Hardly new. It's been like six months, right?"

"Somewhere around there," I say simply, but he's already making a face. "But still, I hate when people talk."

"Ah, fuck 'em," he says before bringing my hand up and kissing the back of it. "Do you care what they think?"

"That I'm sleeping with my hot nanny? Yes, I do care."

He scoffs. "Well, just correct them that I'm the manny."

I roll my eyes. "Because that makes it so much better."

He wags his brows at me before sending me a wide grin. "Do you like sleeping with me?"

I give his face a deadpan stare. "Well, duh."

"Well, I love sleeping with you, so I don't care what anyone thinks."

A grin pulls at my lips as I watch the side of his face. "I don't think anyone has ever said they love sleeping with me."

He gives me a look. "Because you haven't been with a real man."

"Oh?"

"Nope. Scumbags."

I smile. "I've only slept with Simon."

He shakes his head. "So depressing to waste all those years of fantastic hot sex on someone who didn't appreciate you."

I'm breathless. "Fantastic? Hot? My, you know how to make a girl blush."

He kisses my hand once more before turning the wheel as we stop on his street. While I had clothes and a toothbrush, he did not, and he wanted me to ride with him to go back to his house. I have nothing else to do, maybe some numbers I need to input for work, but he promised he'd rub my back while I do it later.

I'm not one to turn down an incredible offer like that.

But even with all that and the promise of great sex later, I am still a little worried about my neighbors possibly seeing Lincoln's car this morning. I highly doubt they'd call Simon, but that would be my luck. I don't want the boys to find out this way. Hell, I don't want to tell them at all yet. We need to wait, but I'm unsure if Lincoln will accept that. If the last twenty-four hours showed me anything, it's that Lincoln has a hard time keeping his hands to himself.

Not that I mind.

I sort of like it.

A-fucking-lot.

Shaking my head at my school-girl feelings, I look up at his condo as we pull into his driveway. I won't bring up my neighbors or anyone else again. He doesn't seem to care, and I probably shouldn't either. But I do. I just don't want anyone in my business. Even if I don't know what that business entails except for phenomenal sex. For one thing, I don't want Simon getting in the middle of it and imploding my world any more than he already has.

When Lincoln's phone chimes again, I'm convinced it

may be more annoying than my ex. It hasn't stopped going off! Making a face, I glare at the phone. "Not to sound like a crazy person, but who the hell is texting you so much?"

He scoffs. "It's the kids I used to care for. We're in a group text together."

"Oh," I say, feeling a little stupid. I knew that, and I should appreciate that he still loves the kids, even though he doesn't see them anymore. "That's sweet."

"Yeah, I miss them a lot." I can hear the yearning in his voice, but when he glances over at me, he smiles. "But I have to say, I've never been this happy."

My heart soars as we share a smile, and he shuts off the car. He kisses my hand once more before pushing the door open, and I do the same. Looking over at me across the top of the car, he glares. "Can you not wait?"

I scoff. "No one does that anymore."

"I do," he says simply, shutting the door. "So wait."

A grin pulls at my lips as we head to the house. Wrapping his arm around my shoulders, he unlocks the door before shutting it behind him. When he presses me into the door suddenly, I gaze up at him as he captures my jaw in his hand. "I want you."

I'm breathless once more. "Oh."

"Yeah, so take a shower with me?"

His question is so out of the blue, I can't help but laugh. "I just took one!"

"So?" His eyes are blazing, the gray such a lovely light color as he threads his fingers with mine, pulling me to him as he holds my hand behind my back. "Just think, all wet and soapy. Fuck, I'm hard just imagining it."

I feel him hard against my gut as I gaze up into his eyes. He absolutely amazes me. Reaching between us, I take him in my hand through his jeans, sliding my hand up and down him. "I don't think I can keep up with you."

His eyes darken. "Oh no, baby, it's me keeping up with you."

My face breaks into a grin as he walks backward, pulling me with him to the stairs. Before we even get up one step, though, his mouth takes mine, and I cling to him. I may not know what we are doing or what we are, but I honestly don't give two fucks at this point.

I don't want to be anywhere but with him.

He turns me so my back faces the stairs and then slowly lowers me down and covers my body with his. Pressing his cock against my hot center, he growls at me, and I bite his lip. "I'm going to fuck you on every inch of my house."

"Oh yeah?"

"Yeah."

But before he can take my lips, someone knocks on the door. We pause, his eyes locking with mine. Shrugging when we don't hear anything else again, he covers my mouth with his. Then we hear, "Lincoln!"

My eyes widen.

It's Phillip.

He looks down at me, his eyes mirroring mine as I scramble underneath him, trying to get up from the stairs. When my head comes down hard on his knee, he winces as he covers my mouth with his hand to keep me from screaming out. My eyes plead with his, but he just shakes his head. "He won't come in," he whispers, but even I know that's not true.

When I hear the doorknob shaking like someone is putting a key in, I smack his hand away, and I take off up the stairs. I really don't want to face my brother–in–law when I am dripping in afterglow from amazing sex with his best friend.

Riana can know, but I am not ready to tell Phillip.

"Hey," I hear Lincoln say.

Phillip makes a noise of contempt. "I knocked."

"I know. I was coming."

Silence. I'm unsure what is happening, but then Phillip says, "I wanted to come by to let you know why my wife kicked me out of the house today."

My eyes widen. That's not good.

"What? What did you do?" asks Lincoln.

"Oh, I did nothing. You did."

Shit. Shit. Shit. Shit.

"Huh? What the hell did I do?"

Phillip laughs. "The one thing I told you not to do."

I cover my mouth because I'm pretty sure I know what that is.

But Lincoln continues to play dumb. "What?"

"Sleep with my sister-in-law."

Well. Crap.

# CHAPTER NINETEEN

## LINCOLN

Phillip is not happy with me.

I'm pretty sure he wants to hit me.

"Um—"

"Don't um m—" He pauses when something moves up stairs. Looking at me with narrowed eyes, he shakes his head. "Hey there, Vera."

I bite into my lip, kind of hoping she plays dumb, but no such luck. "Hey, Phillip."

I can hear the embarrassment in her voice, and I almost want to say something, but I'm pretty sure if I do, he'll deck me.

I am the one who fucked up.

He nods his head in such a stoic and scary way. "Let's go outside."

"Outside?"

"Yeah, it's the space on the other side of the door."

I give him a deadpan look, but he just glares.

"Fine."

He pulls the door open, and I look up the stairs, where Vera is looking down at me, her eyes wide. "I'll be back." She only nods, and I send her a grin. "It's fine."

"It doesn't sound like it is."

"It isn't," Phillip says then, and I inhale audibly, which results in him cutting me one hell of a look.

He is going to kick my ass.

Following behind him, I shut the door before readjusting my pants. Even with the thoughts of my best friend beating my ass, I can't stop thinking of Vera's wanton body against mine. Last night had been one of the best. We just fit, and while I know it's a little early and jumping the gun, my feelings for her do nothing but continue to grow.

When he stops at my driveway, his car behind mine, I tuck my hands into my pockets. I know he is about to tell me off, and I deserve it, but surely when I tell him how I feel, he'll back off.

Won't he?

"Listen, I'm sorry for breaking my promise to you, but this thing between us just clicks, dude, and—"

"Are you a fucking idiot?" He throws his hands up.

"Dude—"

"No, listen to me," he says, coming closer to me, his voice lower than I've ever heard it go. "When I said that I was worried about her and her issues, that is true, but my concerns are mostly about you."

My brows pull together. "Huh?"

"Dude, you understand that this would never work, right?"

I think otherwise, but instead of saying that, I say, "I never said—"

"No, okay?" He's shaking his head. "Don't try to play dumb with me. Riana is on to you."

I laugh, but when he doesn't join in, I press my lips together. "On to me?"

"Yeah, she says that you are feeling Vera more than just fucking around with her. She just wanted this to be a fuck, but now she regrets that because we both know this isn't good."

I'm a bit dumbfounded. "Riana wanted us to fuck? And how do you know that?"

"Riana told Vera to fuck you, but then when Vera did, she freaked out because she felt something for you."

That made me smile a little too big. "Oh, really?"

"Dude!"

I shrug. "What? What's so wrong with that? Am I not worthy of her love?"

He glares. "This isn't funny, man. Honestly."

His words are tight, and he has such a pained look on his face. Giving him a look, I ask, "What is the big deal? We're both adults, and we like each other. I don't see why it's—"

"The big deal is she just got out of a fifteen-year relationship, Linc. She's thirty-one years old. Her boys will be out of the house before you know it."

I'm confused. "Why does any of that matter—"

"You want kids." He says it with so much emotion behind those three words that my heart stops. "You want the wife, the kids, and the dog, for crying out loud. Do you really think she'll want to start over? Think about that, Lincoln, seriously. She comes with all the baggage known to man. Asshole ex, kids with emotional issues, and she works all the damn time."

"I can handle that fuckface, Simon, and the boys are amazing. She works, but she is also doing everything she can to make time for her family."

He doesn't agree. "She's not right for you."

"I think she's perfect for me," I decide, my eyes never leaving his, even though his words hurt.

Because they're true.

He shakes his head, though, almost violently. "No, Linc, you're distracted by the sex, by the fantasy in your head of her being all those things. She won't be, though. She's done with that part of her life. Now she wants to raise her kids and be happy."

All this astonishes me. Where does he get off? "How do you know?"

"Because I know her. She'd probably laugh in your face if you asked her if she wanted any more kids or if she has plans on getting married again. She was in a shitty relationship. Why would she want to do all that again?"

"Because it won't be shitty," I snap. I don't mean to get testy, but he's pissing me off. "I would treat her right."

"And I don't doubt that, not even in the slightest, but she will not give you everything you want."

"I mean, it's been a day. How do you know—"

"'Cause I see it in your eyes," he says, his gaze burning into mine. "I fought Riana so hard on that, told her there is no way you'd be feeling Vera so quickly, but it's all right there. I was wrong, and now I have to tell her that."

My heart jumps up in my throat as I look down at the driveway. "It's nothing."

"It's everything for someone who wants to be loved and needed."

I swallow, trying so hard to ignore his words, but it isn't easy.

"Break this off now, while it's fresh and new and no one can get hurt."

I tuck my hands in farther, knowing that won't happen. "I can't."

When I meet his gaze, he looks away, shaking his head. "Come on, Linc. You know this is going to end badly."

I don't know that. "Who says it's gotta end?"

Silence stretches between us until, finally, he groans loudly. "You've always been the romantic between us. It's annoying, especially for a realist who knows this is going to end so fucking bad that I may lose you as a friend."

That knocks the air out of me. Meeting his angry gaze, I shake my head in shock. "Wow."

"Reason being, if she gets attached to you and you break it off with her because she won't have kids with you or marry you, I swear it, man, I'll be done. For the simple reason, I stood out here, looked you in the eyes, and warned you. I told you not to get involved with her, to keep your dick in your pants. I love you, you know that, but I refuse to watch her go through another heartbreak and have it damage my relationship with my wife."

I don't say anything as I look away, but I feel him watching me. When he lets out a long breath, I still can't look at him. Instead I watch as his feet start to walk away, and when his car door slams, I jump a bit. When he starts the truck, I look up, watching as he pulls out. He doesn't spare me even the slightest of looks. His brow is furrowed, and his cheeks are red. I want to say that everything he said is completely untrue and I wasn't the least bit worried, but I would be lying. What if he is right?

I don't want to lose my best friend, but how in the world am I supposed to ask Vera if she wants the things I want when we've been together a whole day?

Plus, are we even together?

I don't want to know if we are or not, because I don't want this to end. I don't want to be told that this is nothing to her but mindless sex. I want to feel that she is falling for me, the way I am falling for her. I want to think we have a future together, because she's just it for me.

But stupid Phillip just put all this doubt in my head.

Something I didn't even need or want.

When the door opens, I turn to see her looking at me. "He's pissed."

I nod slowly, a smile pulling at my lips, though I don't feel it. Walking toward her, I shrug. "Yup. Not a happy camper."

"What did he say?"

"That I should call this off." I reach for her, pulling her against me as I shut the door behind me. She looks up at me, her eyes wide, and in them, I'm unsure if I'm seeing what I want to see and not the truth.

She moves her hands up my chest. "What did you tell him?"

"I told him no."

Her brows perk. "You weren't kidding when you said you've wanted this for a while."

"Nope, I wanted you the moment I saw you, and if we weren't in a room full of the boys and your sister and Phillip, I would have taken you against the door."

She's breathless as she gazes up at me. "While that tickles my loins"—I snort at that, and she smiles widely at me—"I really don't want to come between you two."

"You won't," I say quickly, nibbling on her jaw. "He's just mad 'cause Riana told him and I didn't," I lie, kissing the spots I nibbled. "It's not a big deal."

She pulls back, her hands coming up to cup my jaw. "Are you sure?"

"Definitely."

A small smile pulls at her lips. "I..." She trails off and bites her lip.

I kiss her nose. "What?"

"I don't want to end this."

"You like the sex?"

She laughs out loud, leaning into me as she wraps her arms around my neck. "I mean, it isn't bad."

I nip at her lips. "It isn't."

"But no, it's not that."

"Then what?" I ask, holding her tightly. "My big cock?"

She snorts this time before pressing her nose into mine. "No! Though, again, that's not a bad bonus."

It's me snorting this time as I kiss the side of her mouth. "Then what is it?"

Her eyes lock with mine as she moves her fingers along the back of my neck. "It's the way you make me feel." It's like taking a shot straight to the chest. My lips start to curve just as she beams up at me. "I've never felt like this."

I inhale deeply, kissing her bottom lip. "Me either."

She chews on her lip for a moment, her eyes never leaving mine. "But, would you be okay if we don't tell anyone, not yet at least?"

My brows come together. "I wasn't going to scream it from the rooftop, but I don't want to act like there is nothing here."

She threads her fingers through my hair. "It's just so much change has already happened for the boys. If they find out I'm dating their nanny, I'm worried it will be déjà vu for them, and I don't want to do that to them. I can't do that." Her eyes search mine. "I know it's not ideal, but can we wait a bit? Maybe when they get back from spring vacation with their dad?"

I should say no. I should do as Phillip told me to.

But I can't.

Recklessly, I agree, "Okay."

"Please understand that I don't do this to hide you or anything like that, but I don't want to throw you into the mix and then something goes wrong."

I slowly nod. "It's smart."

She eyes me. "You're upset."

"No, I'm just annoyed with Phillip and..."

"And you want me?"

My lips quirk. "That's a given."

"No, I mean—"

"I know, and yes," I say simply, pressing my nose to hers. "I want to be with you all the time, and all this means is that we're gonna have to find time for each other. Alone time," I add, wagging my brows at her. But she doesn't laugh. Her eyes are full of worry, and that does nothing but worry me. "But it's fine. Really. I understand. The boys come first."

Her eyes soften as she leans her head to mine. "Thank you."

Closing my eyes, I gather her closer in my arms before capturing her mouth in mine. Even though I feel like we have this somewhat figured out, I can't shake what Phillip said, and that worries me.

But my anxiety over the future can't ruin what I'm feeling right now, in her arms with her lips and body pressed against mine.

Pure euphoria.

# CHAPTER TWENTY

## VERA

"So you're mad?"

"No, I'm not mad," Riana says, but I know she is. She's been very standoffish for the last couple days, and it's killing me.

"Phillip is mad?"

"Yeah, but don't worry about it."

But I am. "Will you tell me why?"

"I don't see the point. Like I told him, you two are grown adults. Do as you please."

I chew on my lips as I hold the curling iron to my hair. "Does he not want us together?"

"Vera, let it be. Just have fun."

I don't like the sound of her voice; she's upset, and I hate that I'm the reason for that. Or that we, Lincoln and I, are. She's pregnant, and she shouldn't be worried about my affairs. I tried asking Lincoln for more details about what had happened with Phillip, but he was tight-lipped. I just want to know what is pissing off my brother-in-law, because I feel good with what's happening with Lincoln.

Very good, and I just want everyone else to feel the same.

"So you won't tell me?"

"I don't see the point of upsetting you when you've had enough of that. It's stupid, and he's probably just jealous."

I think that over for a moment. I know they're the bestest of friends, but still—didn't Phillip want me to be happy? "Okay."

"Okay, I gotta go."

"Oh. All right."

"Bye." She hangs up before I can say more, and my heart aches a little. I want to know what is going on, and it's driving me crazy. I have a feeling I'll have to get it out of Phillip. Which I'm sure will be very awkward.

Glancing in the mirror, I realize I took a little longer on my hair than I normally do. I'm not sure why I'm worried about it, but knowing that Lincoln is downstairs, caring for the boys, I want him to find me irresistible after our weekend together. I know, that's pathetic, but it is what it is. I haven't had a guy actually like me in a very long time, so I might be craving this a little too much. Which makes me nervous. Am I really into Lincoln? Or is it because he's giving me the attention I so greatly crave?

Spraying my hair down with hairspray, I look at myself once more before heading out of my bathroom and going to my bed. Sliding my pumps on, I turn and find Lincoln in my doorway. Within seconds, his eyes change from that light gray to the stormy ones that drive me absolutely crazy. Taking in a sharp breath, I send him a little grin. "Hey. I was about to come down."

He looks down the hall and then back to me. "Can I come in?"

"Where are the boys?"

"Downstairs."

I give him a warning look. "No funny business."

He chuckles as he comes in, heading right for me. I hold out my hands, trying to stop him, but his lips still reach mine for a quick kiss. "You look really hot today."

My chest flutters. "Thank you."

He kisses me once more, this time on the cheek, before stepping back and hooking his thumb behind him. "Listen, I think you need to talk to Elliot."

My brows pull together. "Elliot? Do you mean Louis?"

"No, I mean Elliot. He's been dragging ass all morning, and then when Charlie and Louis ran upstairs to brush their teeth, he came over to me, grabbed my hand, and leaned into me for a moment. He looked really upset but wouldn't tell me what's wrong."

My heart sinks. "Crap. Okay."

I go to walk by him, but he grabs my hand, stopping me. "He squeezed my hand three times. I see you guys do that a lot. What does that mean?"

I look back at him, my eyes getting a little misty. I knew the boys adored Lincoln, but I never thought they'd love him. How could they not, though? He is amazing. "I love you." His eyes widen, and I laugh. "No, that's what it means."

A small smile plays on his lips. "Well, that has made my day."

I beam back at him before nodding. "Mine too. Now let me go find him."

Elliot isn't upstairs, and when I start down the stairs,

Charlie and Louis are moving around the living room. "Boys, where is Elliot?"

"Kitchen," Charlie calls to me, but before I can finish going down the stairs, he looks back to me. "Hey, Mom, since it's your weekend, can you take me to the movies on Friday?"

I nod, excited that it is my weekend, even with my worry for Elliot. "Of course. What are we seeing?"

He looks away shyly. "Actually, it's for a date."

My jaw drops as Lincoln moves past me, holding his hand up for a high-five that Charlie gives him automatically. "So you did what I said?"

Charlie's face changes into the most beautiful smile I've ever seen. "Yup, it worked, and she was all about giving me her number."

Lincoln slaps his hand to Charlie's. "That's my boy."

My heart is currently in my stomach as I stare at my baby. He used to be just little and innocent, but now he wants to date? And Lincoln is cheering him on?

Ah. One thing at a time.

"We will revisit this later," I say before heading toward the kitchen.

My boy wants to date.

I know what dating entails.

*Gah.*

Ignoring my crazy thoughts, I head to the kitchen. I find Elliot still at the island, messing with his cereal. He does look sad, and I feel guilty for not noticing when he woke up. He was a little quiet last night, but that's Elliot. Nothing new. Obviously, I was wrong.

Sliding the chair out, I sit down beside him. He looks over at me and sends me a fake smile. "Hey, Mom."

I wrap my arm around his shoulders. "Hey, honey. You okay?"

He shrugs. "Yeah, fine."

"You sure? Lincoln says he thinks something is wrong, and you look as if something is bothering you."

He looks away, shrugging once more. "It's nothing."

"Well, why don't you tell me, and maybe we can fix it?"

"We can't fix it," he says and inhales before looking back at me. "If I tell you, you'll yell at Dad, and he'll get mad."

*Shit.* I watch Lincoln move around the kitchen to the sink. When I detect movement behind me, I look to see the boys standing in the doorway. Clearing my throat, I say, "Well, how about I promise not to get mad and call Dad?"

His shoulders move again, but he doesn't glance at me. "Dad hates Lincoln."

I'm not surprised, but it infuriates me that he would tell the boys that. When I glance to Lincoln at the sink, I notice his back is taut as he violently washes the dishes. "Why do you say that?"

"Because."

"Because why?"

"He said so."

"Oh," I say, wishing like hell Simon would treat me with the same respect I do him. I don't talk about Kaia in front of the boys, and I sure as hell don't talk about him to them. It's what co-parents do. He's such an asshole.

"He said that you hired Lincoln to replace him," Louis

says then, and I look back at him just as Charlie punches him in the shoulder.

Before I can get on him, Lincoln's voice booms through the kitchen. "Don't hit him."

"Sorry," Charlie mutters to Louis, but then he looks to me. "But we know this will cause a fight; plus, I'm pretty sure Dad is just jealous."

"Okay," I say calmly. "But you all know that's not true. I hired Lincoln because he is a good fit for us."

They all nod, and I feel Lincoln watching me.

"We know that," Elliot says. "But he makes it seem like we can't have Lincoln and him in our lives."

Oh, that man makes me stabby. They're babies! Why put that on them? "Well, again, that's not true. Lincoln will be here as long as he wants to be and we want him. Dad will never leave; he is your dad," I stress, moving a piece of hair out of Elliot's eye. "As for me, I'm yours for forever."

That gets a grin out of him. "I know, Mom."

"Good, so don't you guys worry. You can love all of us, and it's okay. I know Kaia means a lot to you guys—"

"Nope," Charlie mutters.

I glance back to him, glaring. "And that's fine because she is your stepmom. You can love who you want, as long as you love me the most," I say, pressing my nose to Elliot's.

He beams at me, brushing his nose against mine. "Done."

My heart soars, though it's aching so bad. I hate the pain this is causing my boys. I just want them to be happy kids. When Louis comes and hugs me tightly, I kiss their heads. "And don't worry, I won't tell Dad we talked."

"Thanks," Elliot whispers as he slides his hand into mine, squeezing it three times. When his little brown gaze meets mine, I smile before kissing his nose.

"Now, go brush your teeth."

He nods before hopping off the barstool and taking his bowl to Lincoln. When Lincoln takes it, he stops Elliot, chucking him under his chin with his thumb, a grin on his face. Elliot returns the grin before running off. When Lincoln looks back to me, my heart is in my throat.

Oh, this man will be the death of me.

"Okay, well, I'm late," I say, getting up and moving my hands down my dress.

"Can I go Friday? I want to tell her," Charlie says.

"Tell who?" I say, and then I hold my hand up. "Girl. Date. Ugh. Give me a little time to process that."

"Her name is Crystal."

I make a face. "Okay, give me a bit."

"But Mom! Lincoln is so cool about it. Be cool."

I take him by his jaw. "Lincoln also didn't go through nineteen hours of labor with you, so he doesn't know what this is doing to me." I kiss his nose, but he is giving me a dirty look. "We'll talk about it tonight."

"Mom!"

"Charlie, let her think about it."

We both look back at Lincoln, and I wait for Charlie to pop off, but he doesn't. Instead he nods. "Sorry, but she's really great, Mom, and you can come to the movie with the boys and sit seven rows back."

I scoff. "Seven?"

"Yeah. I can't be seen with you guys."

That makes me laugh as I shake my head. "We'll talk later," I say, kissing his head. When I go to reach for my purse, Lincoln is holding it, along with a peanut butter bagel.

"I'll carry this out for you."

My lips curve. "How nice. Thank you."

Together, we walk out, and when he shuts the door, I glare at the sidewalk. "Stupid Simon. I hate him."

"I know," Lincoln agrees as we head down the walkway. "I don't understand his deal."

"I don't either. It's wrong to put all that on our boys."

"It really is, but you can't say anything."

"He's one lucky asshole for that," I sneer, throwing my door open. I sit down as he hands me my stuff.

"Hey, don't let this ruin your day."

"Oh, no," I say dryly, and he glares. "It's not like I have anything else to worry about. My oldest wants to date, my youngest is worried his dad will hate him if he likes you, and I have a huge meeting today. Yup, nothing to worry about." I know he is trying to help, but I feel like his feelings are hurt in a way. I know mine would be. So I wave him off. "Don't worry about it. It's fine. I'm fine. I'll text you when I get to the office."

"You sure?" I nod as he bends down, holding my breakfast sandwich to me. "It's gonna cost you."

I grin before looking to the windows. When I don't see the kids, I give him a quick kiss.

"I want more than that."

"Well, you're gonna have to wait."

"What if I can't?"

I laugh. "The struggle is real."

He laughs as I shut the door once he is out of the way. Watching Lincoln as I pull out, I wish I could tell him I am also worried about what is going on with Phillip.

But he doesn't need to know that.

And he sure as hell doesn't know I'm calling him.

When my brother-in-law's voice comes over my speaker, I don't give him time to say anything before I ask, "So why can't Lincoln and I date?"

He pauses, and it's almost like I can hear him thinking. "Are you sure you want to know?"

I don't hesitate. "I do."

"Fine."

But everything he says is far from fine.

And I'm not sure how that makes me feel.

# CHAPTER TWENTY-ONE

## LINCOLN

I am dying for her.

Sitting on Jenny's couch, I inhale hard as I take in the photo that Vera just texted me. She is wearing the same shirt she left in, but of course, she unbuttoned a few buttons just for me and put a little kitten grin on her face as she looked at the camera. She is stunning, and I'm utterly blown away.

*You won't take the shirt off, huh?*

*LOL! No!*

*Come on, I haven't had
you in over a week.*

*The boys leave this weekend.
You can have me all weekend long.*

I grin, though I know she can't see me.

*So you still want me?*

*What kind of question is that?*

*You've been a little standoffish.*

*Oh? I didn't realize. I'm sorry.*
*Let me hump you in front of my boys.*

I snort in laughter, which earns me a nasty look from my working sister.

*You know what I mean.*
*Usually you at least flirt with me.*

*I've done no such thing, but nonetheless, yes,*
*I want you. I've just been stressed. You do*
*remember I took my son on his first date.*
*It was painful.*

I laugh out loud, and this time Jenny glares at me. "I'm on the phone!"

I mouth *sorry* before looking back at my phone.

*Hardly. He had a great time and got*
*himself a kiss at the end of the night.*

*Thank you so much for that reminder.*
*Remind me of this when I'm going down*
*on you this weekend. SO I DON'T!*

I fight back my laughter.

*You wouldn't hold out on me.*

*Maybe not, but still. We're good, aren't we?*

*I hope so.*

*We are.*

Setting my phone down, I can't help but feel like something is off. It isn't that I don't think she digs me anymore. I know she does, but it's like she's walking on eggshells, or maybe it's that she's not as into me as she was. But we have both been busy as hell this week. I don't know, maybe it's just my insecurities, but one thing is for sure—I want to get her in bed. I want to get her naked so we can really talk. The sex is amazing, don't get me wrong, but talking to her, feeling her against me, that's what I crave.

Us. I crave us.

"Still fucking your boss?"

I look up to Jenny, popping Lincoln to the second power's pacifier back into his mouth. I nod. "I am having sex with my girlfriend, yes."

She rolls her eyes. "You're so dumb."

"Why is that?"

She holds my gaze. "Is Phillip still not speaking to you?"

I look away, shrugging. "No, he isn't."

"So you chose ass over your best friend?"

"No, I want ass and my best friend, but Phillip is being a jerk."

"For good reason. He's right."

I shake my head. "He isn't. Vera is great."

"I don't doubt that, but she's older."

"She's only three years older than me."

"And she already has kids."

"So? Doesn't mean anything."

"It means everything, and you know it."

I roll my eyes, tucking my phone into my pocket before picking up Lincoln. "I'm not having this out with you," I say, going to her and laying him in her lap. "I gotta go get the boys."

She just gives me a dry look. "All fun and games until someone gets hurt."

I don't even entertain her as I kiss her head. "Love you."

"Love you too," she sings. "But you should call Phillip."

I ignore her as I go out the back door. I know she's right about Phillip; I miss him, but he is being a baby. If anything, I am more inclined to believe that Vera and I go together great. When we aren't texting, we're talking on the phone or sending each other pictures. We are enjoying each other. A lot. And our FaceTime sex is so fucking hot. I thought porn was great, but seeing Vera pleasure herself does nothing but take me back to our first time together.

I like her. Hell, I may even love her.

Crazy, I know, but when you know, you know.

But I find myself dialing Phillip's number as I head toward my car. I don't like listening to my sister, but I also don't like the thought of "choosing ass over my best friend." It isn't like that, and I have to make sure he knows that.

"Hello?" His voice is tight. He doesn't want to talk to me.

"Hey, man. What's up?"

He hesitates for a second. "Nothing. Just at work."

"Oh, well, long time no talk."

"Yeah," he says slowly, and I swear it's like pulling teeth.

"So what's been up?"

"Nothing. Just getting ready for the baby, hanging with Riana and all."

"That's cool."

"Yeah."

"Yeah." I tap the wheel with my thumb. "Listen, dude, I miss you, and I don't like that we're fighting."

He doesn't answer right away. "I don't either, but I stand by what I said."

"I understand that, and I don't blame you, but I don't want that for Vera. I don't want to hurt her. I want to be with her. Wholly."

He lets out a long breath. "Man, it isn't that easy. She isn't ready for that kind of thing."

"Did she tell you that?"

"Well, no, but I know her—"

I'm over this "I know her" shit. "Listen, until she tells me otherwise, I'm doing this."

"But you're setting yourself up for failure."

"Then that's on me."

"But don't you see? I'm trying to protect you from that."

"I don't need protecting, Phil."

"I know this, but it's not just you. It's the boys, it's Vera, and if you two split, how will that go?"

I don't know, so I don't answer. In my mind, I don't see an end for us, but what if Vera does?

"Have you talked to her?" asks Phil. "Have you asked what she wants from this?"

"Well, no, but it's only been a little over a week."

"It doesn't matter. If you're in it for the sex, then be honest about it, but if not, then something needs to be said."

I make a face. "So when you and Riana got together, you said, 'Hey, I want you more than sex'?"

He scoffs. "No, but then she wasn't newly divorced with three kids."

I think that over. He is right. "I don't know, but I don't want this to end."

"But you won't talk to her about it because you know she may only be in this for the sex, and you don't want to face that."

I smack the wheel, and damn it, I don't want to think about that. That isn't an option for me. "I don't think that at all. We have a connection."

"Yeah, sex."

"You don't know that."

"Fine, but I stand by what I said."

I shake my head. "Fine. I just wanted to let you know, I didn't choose her over you. You're my brother from another mother, and I can't lose your friendship, but honestly, I think I may be in love with her."

He mutters a curse, and I close my eyes. Clearing his throat, he says, "If that's the case, then talk to her. Make sure you're both going to be good."

I inhale deeply, and even though he can't see me, I nod. "Fine. I will this weekend."

"Good."

"Great. Want to get a beer tonight at Tips?"

"Yeah. Six okay?"

"Great."

When we hang up, I'm smiling. I'm not saying we're good, or even where we are, but he will always be my brother.

Brothers fight—I know that for a fact.

But even so, I'm worried that he may be right. I don't think he is. I truly feel something for Vera, but still, it worries me. What if my fears of her being standoffish are real, and she is only in it for the sex?

*Fuck me.*

Trying to push aside my thoughts, I head to the boys' school. When I pull up, I watch as Elliot and Louis smack each other while Charlie tries to hold them apart. Leave it to them to make me grin.

Rolling the window down, I yell, "Cut it out!"

They separate immediately, looking at me guiltily as Charlie shakes his head. "They're insane," he says before getting in the car. "Fighting over a Pokémon card."

I scoff. "Hey now, Pokémon is life." He gives me a dry look as the boys get in. "How's Crystal?"

"They kissed!" Elliot chimed in with a big grin on his face.

"Yeah, with tongue," Louis adds, and Charlie sinks down lower in the car.

I just beam at him. "First kiss?"

"No!" he shrieks, his voice breaking, making the boys laugh harder.

"Yes! With tongue!"

"I hate you guys," he yells, trying to punch them, but I push him back in the seat.

"I remember my first kiss." Charlie groans, and I laugh. "It's something you never forget."

"Was yours wet? 'Cause they were drooling all over each other," Louis teases, and Elliot snorts.

"He had this goofy look on his face too," Elliot adds.

Charlie groans. "Please, stop."

The boys and I laugh as Charlie slowly dies in the seat beside me. He looks at me, his face red with embarrassment. I squeeze his shoulder. "We're just teasing you."

He doesn't look very pleased as he types away on his phone, but it's part of having siblings. I remember my sisters always giving me shit.

Hell, Jenny still does.

I turn out of the school as Elliot asks, "Do you have a girlfriend, Lincoln?"

I'm a little taken aback by his question, and I'm not sure if I should lie. It seems like the best option, though. "No, I don't."

"Why?"

"Haven't found anyone yet."

Elliot thinks that over. "Mom is single."

"Ell! What the heck!" Charlie groans.

I smile. "I know, bud."

"You should date her."

Louis takes in a quick breath, and Charlie's face scrunches up. "Lincoln doesn't like Mom!"

"Why wouldn't he!" Elliot argues back. "Mom is really pretty."

"She is," Louis says simply. "But she's Mom."

"Yeah, but she should get to go on dates and get tongue-kissed."

Oh, Vera would die right now.

Charlie shakes his head. "Lincoln is like twenty-one. He doesn't like old women."

I can't help but laugh. "I'm twenty-eight, and your mom isn't that much older than me. Only three years."

Charlie glances at me, his brows pull together. "So you like her?"

"I didn't say that."

"But you didn't deny it."

I laugh. "You know how we dropped your conversation? Let's drop this."

"She likes flowers," Elliot adds.

"And Reese's chocolates," Louis joins in, but I shake my head.

"Guys—"

"What, Lincoln?" Charlie says, his eyes teasing. "We're just teasing you."

I shake my head. I love these boys. Truly. But this was not part of the plan.

Neither was sleeping with Vera.

Or falling for her.

But sometimes it's better to ditch the plan.

# CHAPTER TWENTY-TWO

## VERA

When I walk through the door after a long day of meetings, I'm met with the twins, bouncing beside me, big smiles on their sweet faces. They must have just gotten home; they're both drenched in sweat.

"Charlie kissed his girlfriend today!"

"With tongue."

I make a face. "How wonderful, and not what I needed to hear right now."

They both giggle as they run away just as Lincoln comes into the living room. "Guys, shower!" Still laughing, they run up the stairs as Lincoln glances back at me.

"They're in good moods."

He smiles. "We went for ice cream after practice. Louis scored twice and Elliot once. Charlie scored like a billion times. I stopped keeping count."

I beam. "Well that's nice news."

"Did you hear Charlie got his first real kiss today?"

I moan. "Oh, I heard, and I'm not happy about it." His laughter follows me to the kitchen, where I set my stuff and reach for the mail. It's becoming so natural to have him here.

To be able to talk to him like this. "I don't like that he's growing up."

"I know. I'm sorry." His eyes are playful.

"You're enjoying this."

"Oh, watching you freak out, yes, it's fun."

"Ass," I accuse, and he just grins. I can tell he wants to touch me—he's got that burning look in his eyes—but I know he won't. I had been worried about it, but he's actually been great around the boys.

Always the professional.

But I'd be lying if I didn't say I wanted him just as badly.

"So more funny stories."

I glance at him as I open a bill from my credit company. "Hit me with it."

"Elliot decided we should date."

My face scrunches up. "Oh really?"

He laughs. "Yes, because you're pretty, and I need a girlfriend or something, but Charlie says I don't date old women."

"Wow, thanks spawn of mine."

He scoffs. "It is a hoot for sure. They're wonderful kids."

"They are," I agree, opening another bill. "Is that why you're in a good mood too?"

"I'm in a good mood because I'm looking at the most beautiful woman I've ever seen."

My lips purse as I cut him a look. "Such a flirt."

He leans in closer. "Can I take you on a date tomorrow?"

"To your bedroom?"

I don't miss the face he makes, but he covers it very

quickly. "Maybe dinner before?"

I eye him. "I don't know. I think I'd rather just go straight to bed."

His eyes sparkle. "Maybe bed, dinner, bed?"

"Or bed, take-out in bed, more bed, and maybe some spa tub?"

His lips purse. "Know how to make me squirm, don't you?"

"It's a talent," I tease, and he smiles before he looks back, since someone is coming down the stairs. It sounds like Charlie. When he appears, I send him a smile. "Hi, my love."

"Hey, Mom," he says, sitting at the island. "What are you guys doing?"

I nod my head to Lincoln as I open another letter. "Lincoln was telling me about your awesome goals today."

He nods. "Easy peasy."

"My superstar."

Charlie loves that, his face lighting up as I meet his gaze. "What's up?"

"What are our plans for tonight?"

"Doesn't matter to me."

"Can we have game night?"

My heart actually skips a beat. He hasn't asked for game night since Simon left. I slowly nod. "Of course we can."

"Cool. Wanna stay, Lincoln?"

Lincoln cups Charlie's neck, squeezing it tightly. "I wish, man, but I have a date with your uncle."

He makes a face. "You know Uncle Phillip isn't gay?"

This time it's Lincoln making the face. "Neither am I."

Charlie scoffs. "Then hey, maybe you should date Mom," he teases.

I look up, rolling my eyes. "Charlie, cut it out."

He laughs as I meet Lincoln's heated gaze, his lips pursing toward me. "On that note, I'm getting out of here. You guys have a nice weekend."

Charlie mumbles something along the lines of having to go to his dad's, which I feel for him, but I'm excited for my weekend because it involves that man right there.

When the boys come barreling down the stairs to say bye to Lincoln, I reach for another envelope as Charlie leans on the island. "Do you need help?"

I smile. "Unless you have money for all these bills, then it's my job."

He smiles weakly, and I return to what I'm doing. I glance at him a few times, surprised he is still sitting there when usually he's hiding from me. "Everything okay, love?"

He looks up to me and nods. "Yeah, I'm fine."

"Okay."

"It's just..."

He pauses, and I glance up to him once more. "Just?"

He struggles with his words as he moves his fingers together. "Do you miss Dad?"

I pause what I'm doing. "No, love, I don't."

"So you don't think you two would ever get back together?"

"I don't," I say without hesitation. "He's moved on."

"But you haven't."

I blink in confusion. "No, but I'm busy with you, Louis, and Elliot, and my job."

He slowly nods. "But are you happy?"

A smile pulls at my lips. "Oh, Charlie, I'm so much happier now than I was before. I can promise you that."

"I feel like you are. You've been smiling a lot."

"I have a lot to smile for. Three wonderful boys, a great career..."

And a really great man who seems to really like me. I can't say that, though.

Not yet.

"But don't you worry about me, my love. It's my job to worry for you, not the other way around."

His eyes cut to mine, and the love in them rattles me to the core. "I'll always worry for you. You're my mom."

I reach out, taking his face in my hand. "I love you so much, Charlie."

He leans into my hand and nods. "I love you too, Mom."

When he gets up, I ask, "So you tongue-kissed Crystal today?"

His head falls back as he groans. "I'm going to kill you guys!"

When he runs off and the twins start screaming, I just shake my head. It's almost like old times. The kids being crazy and trying to kill each other. It's refreshing. I can't help but grin at the fact they said I should date Lincoln. Did they suspect something? Should I be worried? I don't know if they're ready for that. Or maybe I'm stalling because if I tell the boys, then this is real, and it being real scares me.

Because I can get hurt.

But all that goes away when I see a letter from the boys' school.

I know that letterhead; it's from the financial department.

Opening the letter quickly, my heart pounding in my chest, I feel nothing but pure rage.

Simon told the school I was to pay half of the boys' tuition.

"That son of a bitch."

# CHAPTER TWENTY-THREE

## VERA

I didn't sleep.

I was so angry, I couldn't.

Simon is lucky the boys were home when I got the letter. When they went to bed, though, I tried calling him, but he didn't answer.

Fucking coward.

But I knew his work phone.

Lincoln told me to talk to my lawyer first, but there is no need. I am not obligated to pay this, and I won't. Lincoln tried to calm me down; he even gave me a back rub until he heard the boys coming, but it didn't help. I was furious. Especially after talking to someone at the school that morning.

As the phone rings, I tap my toe to the floor, my eyes wide and full of anger.

When he finally picks up, my voice drops an octave. "You are delusional if you think I'm paying for half the boys' school."

"Vera. How nice to—"

"Fuck you, Simon," I bite out. "How dare you? I called the school. You gave them all my information and told them to come after me for the money? That I was a deadbeat mother who didn't want to pay for my sons' tuition? It's not my fucking job!"

"I can't afford it."

"Then we pull them! That's what normal people do. They don't call the kids' school and badmouth the mom to them! I have to face these fucking people more than you do. How dare you?"

"You're blowing—"

"I am a great fucking mother, Simon, and you know it. That's why you're doing this, because if I won't pay it, it's more change the boys will have to go through. You know I don't want that, so you're trying to make me the bad guy."

"I mean, if the shoe fits."

"You son of a bitch. I'm not paying! I will pull them and blame it all on you."

"And I'll say it isn't my fault. Since you're doing the pulling, I'm sure they'll believe me."

My jaw drops. "Why are you doing this to me? I wasn't the one who left you; you left me. I don't understand why you are making my life so hard."

"Because I hate you."

I hate how surprised I am at the statement. It is so out of the blue. "Well, please, don't fucking hold back."

"You were never there for me—"

"Because you were fucking anyone with tits, Simon. Instead of being with me—"

"You worked all the time!"

"After the fifth time you cheated, yeah, I did go to work. I had to, but even so, I'm a good mom just as you're a good dad, and I don't know why you want to do this. Why you want to fight with me. Can't we just raise the boys?"

"No, because you're trying to replace me!"

"Oh, for the love of God."

"I bet you're fucking him."

"Jesus, Simon. Are you that jealous of him? He doesn't want to be you. He doesn't even care about you. All he cares about is the boys."

"They're my boys, and all they do is talk about him. Lincoln this, Lincoln that, Lincoln loves this. It's fucking annoying."

"So because the boys actually like the nanny, you are treating me like shit? I don't understand why. He isn't replacing you—"

"You have to be fucking him to back him up this hard."

Pinching the bridge of my nose, I inhale deeply. "Even if I were, I wouldn't admit it to you. And another thing—none of this has anything to do with the fact that you have to pay for the school if you want them to go there. I'll have Lincoln homeschool them. I don't care."

He scoffs. "He isn't qualified for that."

"Actually, he is. If you read all the paperwork I sent you on him, you'd know that."

"I won't approve that."

"Well, I won't take them out of a school and put them in a new one when I have the option. So you can pay this, or Lincoln can homeschool. The ball is in your court."

He growls in frustration. "You're the one making this hard."

"No, you are, and for the first time, it's my turn to say, I'll take you to court over this."

"You fucking bitch."

I glare. "If that's all—"

"You know what? I don't know why I thought he would fuck you—you're awful. Boring. Worthless. Which is why no one wants you. They never have. That's why I had to always take care of you. Out of fucking pity."

I press my lips together. "We have nothing else to say—"

The line goes dead.

Biting on my lip, I close my eyes as I let my head fall to the desk.

Why do I let his words hurt me so badly? I know none of it is true, but I can't shake his nasty words. And what bothers me the most is now I'm thinking about Lincoln. What if he is with me because he feels sorry for me?

But I know that isn't true.

I try not to think of what Phillip told me, because it scares me. I mean, it is so early... How in the world could Lincoln even be thinking of forever with me? Wouldn't he get bored of me? What if I am worthless and awful? What if he just really likes being in bed with me, and when things get hard, he runs?

Cheat on me.

I hate Simon.

For he could be the reason I lose Lincoln.

◆ ◆ ◆ ◆

When a knock comes at my door, I look up and ask, "Yes? Come in."

I fully expect it to be my assistant or even Richard, but

when Lincoln pops his head in, my face breaks into a grin. "You."

"Hey. Is this the fancy dancy Ms. Woods's office?"

I stand up, coming around the desk as he comes in holding a big vase of roses.

"Because if it is, her boyfriend came to cheer her up."

Her boyfriend...

Oh wow.

I want to say it's the roses that have me gasping for air, but it's him. He blows my world to smithereens. He comes toward me, and I'm in awe of him as he sets the vase on my desk. "I mean, you said you worked all the time, but I didn't know you were like hot shit here."

I scoff. "I'm not."

"Yeah, you are. I asked to see Ms. Woods, and everyone straightened up when I said your name."

I grin back at him. "Oh, it's nothing, but Lincoln, these roses are stunning."

"Nah, you are," he says, pulling me into his arms as his mouth comes down on mine. I haven't kissed him in what seems like forever, and hell, I missed his lips. Melting into him, I deepen the kiss, needing it. Pulling away, he takes my chin between his forefinger and thumb. "You've been crying."

I swallow hard. "No."

"Liar, I can tell. Your makeup is gone."

Holding his gaze, I try to think when Simon even noticed I had cried. He hadn't, and most of the time it was because of him, but Lincoln noticed. "Simon is a dick."

"Well, I know this."

I shrug. "He called the school and told them I was a deadbeat mom."

His brows pull together. "When did you find that out?" He moves a piece of my hair behind my ear.

"I called on my way in."

"What a jackass."

"Exactly," I say softly, moving my hands along his chest. "It's been a shitty morning. He said some shitty things."

He moves his hand into my hair, tipping my head back. "Like what?"

I shrug, not wanting to tell him.

"Tell me."

I swallow hard, looking down at his chest. "That he pitied me, which is why he stayed with me for so long. Said I was boring and worthless. Just a bunch of bullshit."

"Right. Bullshit. You know none of that is true."

I look up at him and want to ask him if everything Phillip said is true. But I don't think I want to know. At least not this way. All I know is that he likes me and wants to be with me. But what if Phillip is right and my fears of Lincoln changing his mind are true? It absolutely rattles me, and I hate that. "He just fucks with me. That's all."

His eyes burn into mine as he tips my head back, kissing my jaw. I want to ignore my crazy thoughts because when he looks at me like that, I have to believe he wants to be with me. But I was with a man who cheated left and right but looked me in the eyes like he loved me.

So what do I know?

"Want me to make it all go away?"

My body catches on fire. "How do you propose to do that?"

I'm breathless as his beard scratches down my neck. "I could take you right here, on this desk."

When he bends down, taking me by the back of the knees, I wrap my arms around his neck. "Lincoln!"

He chuckles against my mouth as he sits me on the desk. "I could eat you right here, make you scream for me as I lick your clit and suck it into my mouth."

I draw in a deep breath as his eyes bore into mine.

"And then I can take you over this desk, from behind, slamming into you until everyone in this office knows how their boss sounds when she is really excited."

My eyes widen. "You wouldn't."

"I wouldn't?" His lips turn up like the Cheshire cat's.

"You would."

"I would."

And I would let him.

# CHAPTER TWENTY-FOUR

## LINCOLN

I move my hands up her thighs, and my body goes tight from the feel of her sweet thighs on my palms. Her eyes are dark as she grins against my lips, looking so fucking beautiful I can't stand it. I wish that grin never left her lovely face. I hate what Simon does to her. He's such a douche. But she's stronger than she realizes, and I'll always be there beside her, cheering her on.

I sweep my tongue along her lips, and then she scoots to the end of the desk, wrapping her legs around my waist as she opens her mouth for me. I slide my hands up her thighs, taking her ass in them as she deepens the kiss. I have missed her so much. While I know we have the weekend, I can't wait. I need her, and something told me she needed me today.

Pressing myself into her center, I pull my lips from hers, gazing into her eyes as I squeeze her ass. Nothing is said as our eyes stay locked, her fingers playing along the back of my neck while I mold her ass in my hands. I don't know what is happening, but I refuse to let it stop. Moving up her hips, I take her panties in my hands, pulling them down and off her legs before throwing them to the floor. Her eyes are swirling with such desire and heat that my cock strains against my pants.

Holding my gaze, she moves her hands down my body and undoes my pants before taking my cock and running her fingers along the tip of me. Taking in a rough breath, I watch as she puts her heels on her desk, opening herself for me, before guiding me inside her. Disappearing inside her, I groan against her mouth.

Taking her back in my hands, I move into her, so slowly I almost can't handle it. One thing is for sure, her eyes are driving me insane. They're so dark, her face flushing as I move in and out of her. Her pussy so wet and wanton, just for me. Cupping her by the back of the neck, I drink in her beauty as I continue to move into her slowly. I don't want this to end. I want to be right here for the rest of my existence.

Laying my forehead to hers, I move my nose along hers as she squeezes me with her tight pussy. Gasping against her lips, I squeeze her neck as I still inside her. I'm about to blow, and I'm just not ready. When she opens her eyes, her lips parting, I can't stop myself. "You are better than he is." Her eyes widen a bit as I go on. "You are beautiful. Stunning actually, and you deserve the fucking world, Vera. The whole thing." She takes in a breath, her lips pressing to my bottom one, and I don't move. Needing her more than ever. "When it's all said and done, the boys will know who loves them the most and who never bad-mouthed the other. They admire you for your strength just as I do." She brings her hands to my face, moving her thumbs along my beard as I hold her gaze. "You blow me away, Vera. Honestly."

She pulls me closer, her lips meeting mine, and when she

sweeps that sweet tongue along mine, I can't handle it. Holding her by her ankles, I thrust into her, her mouth never leaving mine as I continue to pound into her sweet pussy. She feels like heaven, and with each thrust, I feel myself falling harder and harder for her. I don't know if that's smart since I don't know what she is feeling, but real love isn't a waste of time.

And Vera is no waste of time.

She's everything.

When her lips pause against mine, I gather her in my arms, picking her up off the desk before her legs wrap around me. I thrust up into her as she holds on, her mouth never leaving mine. She kisses me like she never will again. From the combination of her kiss and my cock deep in her, my balls go so tight that soon I can't stop my release. Groaning against her mouth, I jerk up inside her as she squeezes my body with her lovely thighs.

I carry her to the side of the room and press her into the wall as our mouths continue to move with each other, our tongues teasing as our hearts pound in time together. I've never in my life felt so fucking complete, and when I pull back for a deep breath, I almost come once more at the sight of her.

"Stunning."

Her face is flushed, her lips swollen, while her eyes are bright and full of such life. I know I didn't cure her shitty day, but maybe, just maybe, I made it a little bit better.

For she has made my life.

Moving her fingers along my jaw, she cups my face before kissing my nose. "You're too good to me, Lincoln."

I inhale hard. "I can be better."

Her eyes widen. "I don't think I could handle that."

"Well, get ready, 'cause I'm nowhere near done."

A sneaky little grin pulls at her lips. "It means the world to me that you came here today," she whispers against my lips.

"I wanted to make your day."

"You did."

Her lips curve as she presses them to mine and our arms tangle with each other. Fuck, I want so desperately for this to be for forever.

But then we're interrupted.

She pulls back when her phone goes off. She looks at me as she says, "Yeah?"

"Ms. Woods, there is an email from accounting that needs your attention at your earliest convenience."

"I will get right on that," she calls.

When the line goes dead, I smile. "Gotta get back to work?"

She nods. "Unfortunately. Can we continue this later?"

"Absolutely," I say, kissing her once more as I pull out of her, lowering her to her feet.

Looking up at me as I tuck myself back in my jeans, she grins. "Thank goodness I have baby wipes."

I laugh as she heads to her desk and grabs her wipes before cleaning up. "Hey."

She looks up at me, her hands between her legs as she gives me a goofy grin. "Yeah?"

"How do you feel about telling the boys?"

She looks away, her shoulders going tight as she throws the baby wipes away. "I thought we said after they went with Simon?"

I shrug. "I know," I say, buttoning my pants. "But I think they suspect something, and I'm honestly dying not able to touch you when I want."

She smiles as she reaches for her panties. "I am too, but I don't want too much change. Plus, with Elliot feeling like he can't love you and Simon, I don't want him to feel pressured."

I understand that, but still, something is bothering me. "But this is more than sex, right?"

Her brows pull together. "Why—"

Before she could finish, though, her phone goes off once more. "I'm so sorry, Ms. Woods, but now Richard is emailing you, and he wants to see you."

"Yes, sorry, tell him I'm on my way," she says, and when she looks back to me, her eyes are soft. "I'm so sorry. Can we talk later?"

My stomach drops. "Yeah."

She slides her panties up her legs before fixing her dress and coming to me. Going to her toes, she kisses my jaw. "It's more than sex, okay? Just don't rush this."

She kisses me once more before heading past me and out of her office, but I'm standing there, stunned.

*Don't rush this.*

Why would she say that? To me, that means she isn't in it for the long haul.

*Fuck.*

Feeling a little defeated, I turn and head out of her office, my heart pounding in my chest. But am I overreacting? Maybe I'm overthinking this? Maybe she meant not to rush telling the boys. Yeah, that's it.

Right?

*Damn it.*

I nod to the receptionist as I pass, but when I reach the elevators, my phone is ringing. When I pull it out of my pocket, I hope it's Vera asking me to come back, but it isn't.

"Sharron! What's up?"

"Loads, Lincoln. How are you?"

I smile when I hear the kids in the background. "I'm great."

"Well, I'm hoping that you'll be even better when I ask my next question."

I scoff. "What's that?"

"Please come to Germany and take your job back."

My heart stops.

*Holy shit.*

# CHAPTER TWENTY-FIVE

## VERA

Ugh, what a day.

When I walk in the door, I notice the boys' bags by the door, and then I see them on the couch with Lincoln, watching TV. When they all glance to me, I smile at the sight of them. They all look so comfortable, gathered together on the couch with such content looks on their faces.

My boys.

"Hey, guys."

They greet me as I slide my shoes off and set my box of work down. When I stand, Lincoln is there, and my breath catches. I can still feel him inside me, and I want desperately to greet him with one hell of a kiss, but I can't.

"Want me to take that to your office?"

"Please."

"Sure," he says before grabbing it and heading up the stairs. As I watch him, I hear his words from earlier.

*This isn't just sex, right?*

God, why would he even think that? It's been bothering me all day. Tearing my gaze from him, I look to the boys. "What are you guys watching?"

"Basketball."

"Fun," I say dryly as I place kisses on each of their heads. They don't pay me any mind, though. They're too deep in the game. Rolling my eyes, I head toward the kitchen for a nice glass of wine, but before I can get there, the doorbell rings. I make a face as I glance at the time.

That better not be Simon to get the boys.

Turning to go back to the door, I see Lincoln coming down the stairs, his brows pulled together. "You expecting someone?"

"No," I say as I reach for the door. "Not yet, at least."

When I pull it open, Simon is standing there with Kaia. I glare. "You're early."

"Hello to you too," he says, walking by me and pulling Kaia along.

Rolling my eyes, I slam the door shut, and when I turn, Lincoln is glaring, his arms crossed.

"Dad? You're early. We still gotta eat dinner," Charlie says, but Simon shakes his head.

"I'll take you guys to dinner. Go upstairs. I need to talk to your mom."

"But Lincoln cooked," Louis says, getting up. "My favorite, ziti."

"He can save you some. Go on."

The boys look to me, and I hold my hands up calmly. "It's fine. Go on upstairs. I'll have Lincoln make you guys plates to go."

"No, he can leave," Simon says then, and I laugh. Out loud.

"You don't get to decide who stays and goes in my house,"

I say simply before ushering the boys upstairs. Charlie looks up at me, worry swimming in his brown eyes, but I kiss his forehead. "No big deal."

He doesn't look convinced, but I don't feel that way either as they run up the stairs.

When I hear their doors shut, I turn to look at Simon and Kaia. "Let's go in the kitchen," I direct before glancing at Lincoln. "Can you make them plates?"

"It's not done yet. Another ten minutes."

"Okay, that's fine," I say, and I don't want him to leave. "Wanna stay for a drink?"

He nods. "Yeah."

Simon scoffs. "Yeah, you two aren't fucking."

Lincoln's eyes cut to him. "That's none of your fucking business."

Simon snaps his lips shut, and I want to laugh as we enter the kitchen. I go to the other side of the island, offering them the barstools. Kaia sits down, but Simon stands as I cross my arms across my chest. "So? What's up?"

"So about the boys' school." I hold my breath as he pulls out some paperwork from his back pocket. "I've had some new guidelines drawn up."

He lays the papers on the countertop, but I refuse to touch them. When Lincoln hands me a glass of wine, I take it. "It doesn't matter what guidelines you've had drawn up. They are insignificant. I'm not signing anything. I gave you the options."

He lets out a long breath. "I can't afford it. I'm switching jobs."

I watch as Kaia looks down, and my brows pull together.

"Switching jobs? Why would you leave a job that pays as much as the one you have?"

"That's none of your business."

I look to Kaia again, and I know that look. I shake my head. "It doesn't matter where he works. He'll always be a cheater."

"Don't talk to her," Simon bites out, but I don't miss the way Kaia looks at me, such hurt in her eyes.

"Watch your tone, Simon," Lincoln warns, and Simon glares back at me.

Still my gaze is locked with Kaia. I may hate her, but I wouldn't wish what he did to me on anyone. Even the woman he left me for. "Get out while you can."

"Shut up!" Simon yells.

Lincoln holds his hand up, his eyes menacing. "One more time, and I knock your teeth to the back of your throat. You talk civil to her, or you can leave."

Simon laughs. "You don't matter, dude."

"Actually, I do," Lincoln says simply. "You're in her home. Respect her or leave."

Simon looks to me, and I stand my ground. "He's right."

"Yeah, and you're not fucking him."

I've had enough. Slamming my hand to the table, I point to him. "I don't know what your obsession is with Lincoln, but it's getting old," I snap. "If you're jealous, that's your issue, not mine. Live your life, and let me live mine, okay? We are nothing to each other but parents to our boys. We don't even need to talk unless it has to do with the boys. In this instant, you have your options. Choose one, let me know, and we'll go from there. Lincoln is more than ready to homeschool them."

I feel Lincoln's gaze on the side of my face, and when I look to him, he has this look on his face. Almost like he wouldn't do it. I don't understand, but I can't ask in front of Simon. Inhaling hard, I say, "I think we're done here. Nothing will change with the parenting plan from this moment on. Have a nice night."

Simon throws his hands up. "You b—"

"Watch it," Lincoln says, cutting him off. "You won't talk to her like that in front of me."

Frustration is written all over Simon's face, but I have to say, I enjoy that he is scared of Lincoln. When he turns and yells for the boys, Kaia slowly starts to get up, but Lincoln stops her. "Why don't you take this ziti with you?"

She gives him a weak smile. "That would be nice. I'm not up to cooking anyway."

"Sure, hold on," he says, and then he goes to work putting the pan in a travel bag as I look to her.

Her eyes meet mine, and she bites her lips. "I'm really sorry."

"Not your fault."

"No, I mean about what happened. I don't think I ever really apologized."

I swallow hard. "I appreciate your apology." She nods slowly, looking away, and I say softly, "But seriously, Kaia, get out while you can."

When she looks back to me, I can see it in her eyes. She is going to make the same mistake I did and stay.

Poor girl.

When Lincoln hands her the travel bag, the boys come running into the kitchen for me. "Lincoln packed up the ziti for you."

Louis makes a face. "What will you eat?"

I shrug. "I'll manage."

Charlie hugs me. "Make sure you eat and not just work."

I smile before kissing his cheek. "I will."

"I love you, Mom," Elliot says, and I kiss him next.

"I love you. Have a nice weekend."

Walking with them, I notice Simon has already gone to the car, Kaia following behind, carrying the ziti without his help. Lincoln would never allow me to do that, but Simon is nowhere near what Lincoln is.

Shaking my head, I watch the boys wave as they run to catch up before getting in the car. I wave when they look at me, and when the car pulls off, I step back, shutting the door behind me. I wish I didn't have to let them go. I wish I could make Simon go away, and for the first time, I care enough about Kaia that I wish she would get out while she can. No one should go through what I did, but I'll never have to deal with that again.

I'm with a man who would never do that to me.

Or at least I hope he wouldn't.

Where is Lincoln?

"Hey."

"I'm still in here."

"Oh," I say with a laugh. "I thought you'd have attacked me by now."

When he doesn't laugh, my brows pull together before I enter the kitchen to find him behind the island, a glass of wine at his lips. "You okay?"

He looks up at me and clears his throat. "We need to talk."

My heart sinks. "About?"

"A lot of things, actually."

"Being?" I ask as I go to the island, reaching for my wine.

He holds his glass in his hand, swirling his finger along the top, and I feel like he's searching for his words. I'm unsure what is going on, but an uneasiness falls over me. Nervously, I say, "If this is about Simon, I'm sorry. He's a jackass, but I was serious when I said I won't deal with his shit—"

"No, it's not that. You handled that perfectly."

I bite into my lip, pride burning in my chest. I'm proud of myself for saying what I did, but having confirmation from Lincoln makes it ten times better. But I'm worried by the furrow on his forehead. "Okay, then what's wrong?"

Swallowing hard, he glances up at me. "The Ellentons called today."

I smile. "Don't they always call?"

He looks away, and something isn't right. "Yeah, but today was different."

"Why is that?"

He inhales, and his gaze cuts to mine. "They asked me to take my job back."

I swear my heart stops in my chest, but that is silly.

Surely, he wouldn't take it.

"Okay?"

"And I'm wondering if I should take it."

# CHAPTER TWENTY-SIX

## LINCOLN

Vera's lips part as her eyes widen.

I was stressing all day after getting off the phone with Sharron. After promising to call her Monday with an answer, I've been going back and forth on what to do. On one hand, I know with the Ellenton kids I'll have a job and I'll be set for at least ten years, but here, with Vera and the boys, my time is limited.

Unless she wants more with me.

"I'm sorry?"

I lick my lips—they're incredibly dry—and I can't ignore the thump of my heart. "I miss the kids, and they need me. Sharron isn't handling at-home life, and she wants to go back to work. They offered me a lot of money and will pay for me to go over there."

"To Germany?"

"Yeah."

Her eyes narrow. "What about your job here? With my boys?"

"I would stay until you found another nanny."

"But how would the boys handle that?"

"They're doing great, and I'm sure we can find a good nanny for them."

"They love you."

"And I love them," I say, and I mean it, but the more I think about it, the more I can't keep staying here without knowing where we stand. "But this job is a great opportunity, and I've always wanted to see Germany."

"Wow," she says, shaking her head. "I'm sorry, but this hurts."

"I don't want to hurt you—"

"But you are. I mean shit, Lincoln, what about us?"

"What about us?" I ask. I want her to say it. I want her to say she wants me. "I don't know what we're doing, and when I asked earlier, you couldn't answer me."

She gawks at me. "I was working! I told you we could talk later."

"Yeah, but when you said don't rush things, I took that as we're just fucking around."

"I told you from the beginning we weren't fucking around! I told you I wanted you."

"I know, but do you want me for the long haul or just in your bed? Plus, you refusing to tell the boys bothers me. They know, I feel it, and Simon surely knows now, so what's holding you back?"

"I don't know... Timing? I told you I needed time."

"And I need you. All of you. All the time," I blurt out.

When she looks up to me, her eyes are filling with tears. "Leave."

"What?"

"Leave," she says, shaking her head. "I don't want to be around you right now. I thought we were doing something here, but you apparently weren't really here."

"Yes I am!" I yell, throwing my hands to her. "I want this job, but I need a reason to stay here."

Her eyes widen. "I can give you four!" she yells. "Charlie, Louis, Elliot, and fucking me. Jesus Christ, Lincoln. What the hell? You told me I was enough, but apparently I'm not if you're going to leave for a job."

"No, that's not true. I just need to know—"

"Oh really? Because everything you just said seems to mean otherwise!"

I shake my head. "I just want to know if this has a future."

"Then fucking ask me!" she yells, her eyes filling with tears. "Instead of making me feel like my kids and I aren't enough to keep you here. I mean, shit, Lincoln, I've been through that. I thought you were different."

I cover my face. "This isn't what I wanted. I didn't want this to turn into a fight. I just want to know what is going on with us."

"No, you want a fucking out, just like the fucker who cheated on me and left me. Well, guess what. I won't let you hurt me. Get the fuck out."

"Vera—"

"No, leave," she says before throwing her glass in the sink. When it shatters, she doesn't even stop. She stomps out the room, and while I want to chase after her, I know I shouldn't because I just fucked up.

But I'm not leaving.

## VERA

As tears roll down my cheeks, I slam my door shut and lock it behind me for good measure. I can't believe him! I don't understand what he thought would come out of that, but damn it, he just broke my heart! I believed him when he said he was different, that he wouldn't hurt me, but obviously I was beyond wrong.

God, I am such an idiot!

Sitting on the edge of the bed, I cover my face as I cry. I'm embarrassed that I'm crying like this, but I can't help it.

I think I love him.

Gah. I'm so stupid.

I haven't even known him that long, but it just feels right. I don't want him to leave; I want him to stay here, be with me and the boys. Love us. Be with us, but apparently, we aren't good enough.

Again.

As a sob leaves my lips, my mind is going a million miles a second. How will I tell the boys? They love him. So damn much. And how will I ever let anyone else own my heart again? I won't. I will grow old by myself, and when the boys leave me, I'll get birds to keep me company.

Ugh. that isn't the future I want.

I want Lincoln.

The thought of someone loving me, wanting me for forever—it is so appealing.

But that is all over.

Stupid Lincoln.

I shake my head and then wipe my face. I look up at the ceiling, inhaling hard.

I can't believe him.

When the doorknob starts to shake, my eyes widen. "Didn't I tell you to fucking leave?"

"Yeah, but that doesn't mean I'm going to listen."

I glare at the door. "I have nothing to say to you. Leave!"

"No."

"Yes!" I yell, but then I cry out when a foot comes through my door. "What in the hell!"

"I told you I wanted to talk to you," he yells through the hole before reaching through it to unlock the door. "And if I remember correctly, you once told me when you're passionate about someone, you throw baseball bats. So you should appreciate this."

I did, but I wasn't telling him that. "You asshole! You're fixing that!"

He slams the door open after walking through it like he owns it. I stand, glaring at him as he comes to me. "That's fine, because I'll fix everything as long as it means I don't lose you."

I scoff, pointing to the door. "Oh really? 'Cause downstairs you were singing a different tune!"

He throws his hands up in the air. "What can I say, Vera? I'm an idiot! You make me insane!"

"Me? I didn't do anything!"

"You do everything," he yells, closing the distance between us, and there is nowhere for me to go since the bed is behind me. "From the moment I met you, you've made me feel things I've never felt a day in my life. I fucked up, and I know that. But

I have this need to be needed—to be wanted—and I just wanted you to say it. I wanted you to tell me you didn't want me to take the job because you wanted me."

My face scrunches up. "Have I given you any reason to feel like I don't want you?"

"I told you, I feel like you've been standoffish—"

"Because I didn't want to get my hopes up!"

"But my hopes are up too!"

"I know that, but—"

His brows pull together. "Huh?"

"I know they are. I talked to Phillip," I blurt out, and his eyes widen as I cross my arms over my chest, trying to protect my heart. "He told me about the argument you two had, and how he didn't think I was good for you because of all the shit I've been through and then what you want. He told me how you fought to be with me because you felt things for me. It gave me such a high to hear those things, Lincoln. I got so excited, but then I was worried that they couldn't be true. Why would you want me like that when you can have anyone?"

"Because no one is you," he declares, his eyes burning into mine.

I press my lips together, drawing in a deep breath. "The more we talked, the more we were together, it just all felt right. We felt right, and it scared me to the core. And the past couple days, we were perfect, and I was ready to give you my heart, trust you, but then you come at me with that bullshit."

"Because I'm scared too," he says softly. "What if he's right? I swear I ask myself that all the time. I go back and forth with myself, Vera, I do, but the more I think about it, the more

I know nothing else matters but you and the boys."

I want to believe him, I do, but I shake my head. "What about the Ellenton family?"

He looks away, biting his lip. "I won't lie. I love them, deeply, but they aren't Charlie, Louis, Elliot, or you."

Looking away, I close my eyes as he goes on.

"I fucked up. I came at you wrong with what I was feeling, but I was scared, Vera. I kept asking myself, do I stay here, continue to do this and hope that one day you'll feel something for me while I fall harder and harder not only for you but for the boys? Or do I get out before we all get hurt?"

A tear slides down my face, and when he takes me in his arms, I don't have it in me to fight him. I'm scared too. It freaks me out to think of him leaving, but maybe he's right. Maybe he should just go, no matter how wrong it feels.

As tears rush down my face and fall off my chin, I take in a shaky breath and then shrug. "I just don't know, Lincoln—"

"Well, I do."

I look up at him as he slides his hands into mine, tangling our fingers together before taking them behind my back. Pressing his chest into mine, he gazes into my eyes. "Would you want to start over?"

I just blink. "Start over?"

"Well, not really start over, but get married again, maybe have another kid?"

His gaze entraps mine, and I don't dare look away. "I don't know. I have three great kids. Maybe, if it is the right person, but I'm not against it by any means."

"Could I be the right one?"

"Is this before or after what happened downstairs?"

He gives me a dry look. "Now. Right now. Because when I look at you, you're the right person for me. We do feel right. We feel fucking perfect, and I need to know you want me more than for just a bit. I need to know that you have every intention of making this work."

Do I?

Gazing into his eyes, I try to imagine how I would be without him. It's so natural to have him here. To have him care and help me raise my boys. To make love to me, to be there for me, and to listen to me when I have such a bad day. He cares about me, my well-being, and now that I've had that, I don't know if I can let it go.

"Do you want to go to Germany?"

"No."

"Are you sure?"

"Yes. Unless you're going with me, I'm not leaving," he says, pressing his nose to mine. "I will knock down every single door you try to hide behind."

I can't help it; I smile as his eyes burn into mine.

"Because I want to fight every battle with you. I want to stand against whatever storm comes, and I want to raise those boys into fine young men. I want to be there for you. I want to make love to you. I want to be yours and only yours."

Breathless, I almost can't believe him, but again, his eyes say it all. Each word he's said is swimming in his eyes. They're begging me, promising me the world, and I can't look away. When he swallows hard, his eyes glaze over just as he squeezes my hands three times.

And my world stops.

"Really?"

His lips tip as he slowly nods. "Really. I love you, Vera. So fucking much. And while I'm not one to believe in love at first sight, I think you may prove it exists. I've never craved anyone the way I crave you, and I know that won't ever change. I know he promised you that, but I mean it. You complete me, and I know how you need to be loved. Entirely. And that's all I want to do. I want you for forever, and I honestly can't walk away from this. Tell me you can't either."

My heart is soaring, my body shaking, and I don't question his claim. I feel it everywhere—all over my body—and I know I couldn't walk away from him even if I tried. Gazing up into his eyes, my heart jackhammers in my chest as I slowly but confidently squeeze his hands three times.

When his lips curve into the most spectacular grin, I can't help but grin back.

Inhaling hard, I move my lips against his as I whisper, "I can't."

His eyes soften as he gathers me close. "Good. I wasn't going to let you anyway."

As our lips meet, I already know that.

And boy, what a feeling that is.

# CHAPTER TWENTY-SEVEN

## LINCOLN

Vera is freaking the hell out.

Meanwhile, I'm good, but watching as she nervously bounces her leg, I have to hold in my laughter. I am pretty sure the boys are confused, but they sit at the edge of the island, their eyes cutting between Vera and me. They are all sun-kissed and a tad burned from their vacation with their dad, but they look happy. They talked our ears off about how much fun they had, and I could tell that bothered Vera, which only makes me hate Simon more.

But he isn't going away, and I have accepted that.

Still, though, I don't understand how he could afford a vacation yet keep fighting Vera on paying for school for the boys. It's on paper. He has to pay it, but any chance he gets, he bitches. Vera isn't backing down, though. She stands by what she said, and while I agree with her, it would be hard to truly homeschool them when I just started my job at their school as an aide. It was an impulse decision, but I think it just validated what I wanted with Vera.

I wanted a partnership.

Which is what I told Sharron. Thankfully, she understood,

and I planned on going to see all of them soon, but I couldn't work for them. Not when I am completely in love with Vera and the boys.

"What's going on? Why are you being weird, Mom?" Charlie asks.

Vera brings her lip between her teeth. Glancing at me, her eyes widen, and I just smile.

God, I love this woman.

"Well," she says slowly before turning her gaze back to them, "we need to talk."

Louis's brow rises. "About what?"

"Well, sometimes, you see..." She pauses and looks to me for help.

I can't help but laugh. "You're killing me. You said you had this."

She glares. "I'm trying," she mutters.

I shake my head. "Guys, I asked your mom out and she agreed."

The boys' gazes cut to Vera, but she's gawking at me.

"What?" I ask.

"I thought we were going to explain it better!"

"I think it's pretty cut and dry. I like you, you like me, I asked you out."

She gives me a dry look, and I just grin at her. Man, I love driving her crazy.

"You said yes?" Elliot asks, and her eyes widen even more.

"I did."

"So you two are dating?" Louis asks then.

Vera glances to me quickly before looking back to him.

"Yes."

The twins look to Charlie, but his gaze is on his mom. "Are you happy?"

Her shoulders fall, and within seconds, a smile covers her lips as she slowly nods. "Very much so."

All three boys nod, and then Charlie stands before setting me with a look. "Cool. Don't hurt my mom."

"I won't," I say with a grin, and Charlie walks away like it's nothing.

Vera's jaw drops, and I can't keep my grin at bay. She is more nervous about him than the twins, but I think Charlie knows I wouldn't hurt Vera.

Louis looks at me, his eyes narrowed. "We can take you out."

"I'm aware."

When he walks away, following his brother, Elliot looks back at me. "She needs someone to treat her like a queen."

I chuck his chin. "Done."

He nods, sending me a grin before running off after his brothers. I swear those boys are the best kids in the world. I look to Vera, and her eyes are wide once more, and her jaw is basically lying on the ground. "Told you that would be easy."

She shakes her head. "I thought it was going to be bad."

I send her a wink before bringing her into my arms. "They know a good thing when they see one. Me and you, we're good, and no one can ever deny that."

"Phillip and Riana did."

"Correction. Phillip did, but we're making him eat his words."

She beams up at me. "We are. It's kind of fun."

"It is, and just think, we get to rub it in his face for the rest of our lives."

She grins up at me, cupping my face in her hands. "Rest of our lives?"

"Yup, and then some."

As her eyes dazzle into mine, I drop my mouth to hers, feeling my promise deep in my soul.

Right where she belongs.

# CHAPTER TWENTY-EIGHT

## VERA

*A year later...*

Well, shit.

I run my hands down my face, blinking a few times, almost unable to believe what I am seeing.

"Okay."

I head out of the bathroom and pass the bed I now share with Lincoln. I almost can't believe it's been over a year since we decided to do this. Well, really, I don't think either of us actually decided. It's all fate, and I couldn't be happier. When Lincoln moved in three months ago, I was worried the boys wouldn't be able to adjust, but I swear they didn't care. If anything, it made it easier for them to have access to Lincoln whenever they wanted him. Now I'm convinced, most of the time, they love him more than me.

They all get along just perfectly.

And I love it.

But Simon? Well, he is another story.

I wish I could say that things were good between my ex and me, but they aren't. He is still a dick—but a single dick since Kaia left him about six months ago after the second time he cheated on *her*. At least she was smart enough to get out early. I know this because she comes by to let the boys see their little brother. Simon is such a shit dude. It's a shame he keeps having boys. Thankfully there are good men out there who want to help raise his boys to be real men.

Lincoln does it with ease.

And I can't love him enough for it.

Heading down the hall, I call out for the boys, but no one answers me. Looking through their rooms, I don't see anyone. This is weird; they were just up here.

From the stairs, I call, "Lincoln?"

He doesn't answer.

"What in the world? Where is everyone?"

I pat my pockets to find my phone, but I think I left it in the kitchen. I head that direction, looking for signs of life on my way, but the house is empty. What in the world? They were all just here. Did they head out?

They better not have!

Reaching the island, I see my phone with a green sticky note on top of it. I pull my brows together when I see Lincoln's handwriting.

*Come to the front yard.*

I'm confused. Why in the world are they outside? And why couldn't they just call me out there?

Weirdos.

*Oh!*

I pause midstride. I swear if I get hit with a water balloon,

I will kill them all.

I get to the front door and cautiously pull it open. "If I get hit with a balloon, I will lock you all out."

"You threw them away!" Charlie calls.

"And told us we couldn't play with them anymore," Elliot says.

I shrug. "Well, that's what happens when you drench your mom after work!"

"Lincoln did it too!" Louis shouts.

Lincoln laughs. "Just come out here!"

I might regret this, but I peek out. I see Riana and Phillip's car. Confused, I pull the door open more before coming out and heading down the steps. "Riana's here—"

My words fall off when I see all six of them standing on the lawn.

Breathless, I take in what I'm looking at.

Charlie is holding a sign that says *Will*.

Elliot is holding *You*.

Louis holds *Marry*.

And Riana and Phillip hold *Him*, with an arrow pointing to Lincoln.

Tears rush to my eyes as Lincoln comes toward me, a single rose in his fingers, before he stops below the stair I'm standing on.

"Hey," he whispers as my tears start to fall.

"Hey," I say with a laugh.

"Did you read that message?"

"I did."

His eyes sparkle. "Good, 'cause I wrote it." My face breaks

into a grin as he slowly lowers to one knee, his eyes locked with mine. "When I look into your eyes, I don't only see your heart. I see Charlie, Elliot, and Louis—your boys. Boys I've fallen in love with as if they are my own. Vera, I look at you, and I see a strong and beautiful woman who is too good for me, but you still chose me."

A sob leaves my lips as he reaches up, takes my hand in his, and kisses my palm. "I want to raise these boys with you, and they're okay with it. I asked them if I could marry you, and they all agreed that they want me in their lives as a stepdad. Since I want them, and you, I need to lock you in and make you mine because no one else can ever be what you are to me. My missing piece."

"Oh, Lincoln," I gasp, covering my mouth with my hand to keep the sobs in.

He reaches into his pocket and pulls out a little blue box I recognize almost immediately. When he opens the box to a beautiful square-cut diamond, I close my eyes. This can't be real. But when I open my eyes, I see it is.

Gazing up at me, his eyes are misty as he whispers, "So what do you say? Will you marry me?"

Tears gush down my face as I quickly nod. "Of course I will."

He rises to his feet and slides the ring down my finger before gathering me into his arms. He kisses my lips hard and pulls me even tighter to his body before bringing his lips to my ear. I don't hear a thing. Not the boys, who are likely hooting and hollering, or even Riana and Phillip. I'm in shock.

I have it all.

And I am about to give it all to Lincoln.

"I'm pregnant."

He stills in my arms, and I feel his heart jackhammering in his chest. "Did you just say you're pregnant?"

"I did."

He pulls back, his eyes boring into mine. "Really?"

"Yes."

When a tear spills against his cheek, my breath catches. "Well, now I *gotta* marry you."

My face breaks into a grin before he captures my mouth with his. Lifting me off the ground, he kisses me deeply, and I swear I feel it everywhere. When the boys come up to join us, Lincoln puts me down and wraps us all up in his arms. But as we're all squeezing each other, his eyes don't leave mine.

"You continue to give me the world."

My eyes fill with tears. "You give us more than that."

"And that won't ever change," he says, managing to get his hand up to cup my face. "I love you."

"I love you."

He kisses me as we hold our boys, and I feel complete.

After years of thinking I couldn't have it all, I finally do.

And then some.

Three boys who love me unconditionally and a baby on the way.

With the man of my dreams.

My manny.

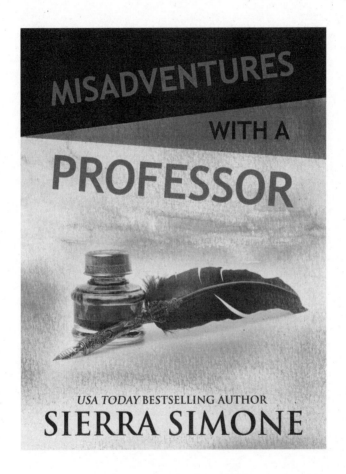

# EXCERPT FROM
## MISADVENTURES WITH A PROFESSOR

She's shivering.

It takes me a moment to notice, as I'm still processing how someone emerged out of this tempest right in front of me. I'm also still processing how this someone in question is a creature made of pale skin, dark hair, and a sinfully red and lush mouth. Like a vampiress straight from a storybook, but with the most incongruously innocent eyes I've ever seen.

She's also young, drenched to the bone, and utterly, utterly inappropriately dressed for a night like this.

"Why aren't you wearing a coat?" I demand over the roar of the rain, and her gaze blinks up at me—which is when I realize she's been staring at my mouth. A kick of heat goes straight to my cock.

I ignore it.

"And why are you barefoot?"

Her eyes flick back to my frowning mouth, and her own mouth parts ever so slightly, as if my bad-tempered scowl fascinates her. Her tongue darts over her lower lip, licking away a bead of rainwater that settled over her fire-engine-red lipstick, and I find I want her to do it again. And again.

And again.

I could watch her licking rain off her lips for the rest of my life.

"I'm looking for the Goose and Gander," she finally offers. It's hard to hear her over the rain, and yet even with the *whoosh* and *churr* of the torrent, I can hear her accent. Broad and wide and a little flat, American television style.

I know where the Goose and Gander is. I just came from there, actually, having endured a meal deconstructed into various mason jars and served on a wooden plank for the sake of seeing some old friends. But I'd drawn the line at overpriced cocktails decanted into chemistry beakers and opted to go back to my hotel instead.

Which is where I want to be—in my dry bed, with dry clothes and dry blankets and a dry book—not in the drenching rain with a barefoot little American. No matter how red her lips are. Or how enticingly her wet dress clings to her frame.

I scowl again.

"It's back that way," I say, pointing behind me. "Just around the corner."

"What?" she asks, clearly unable to hear me.

"It's back that— Oh, fuck it," I mutter, taking her by the elbow and yanking her into the deep doorway of a closed shop. The absence of the rain is almost as shocking as the presence of it, although it still rushes down next to us in a dull, silver roar.

"It's just past the corner there," I say again, and in the sheltered cove of the doorway, she can finally hear my words.

"Left at the lights, then just a street down."

"Oh, good," she says, looking genuinely pleased. And also genuinely cold. Goosebumps pebble her bare arms and chest, and I make a valiant effort not to notice her nipples bunched tight under her dress.

A very valiant effort.

I fail, of course.

Her teeth chatter as she says, "Th-Thank you! My phone wouldn't work in the rain, and I thought I memorized the way, but it all looked different once I actually got here, and then the rain made it so hard to see—" Her own shivers break apart her words, and for some reason this makes me unaccountably annoyed.

"Here," I say gruffly, shrugging out of my jacket and putting it over her shoulders. She's flapping a hand in protest, but her hand stills as soon as the dry, warm interior of the jacket touches her shoulders. She practically folds herself into the jacket then, doing this thing where she rubs her cheek against the collar, and I know it's to get dry—*I know that*—but fuck if it doesn't look like she's nuzzling into it. Like a kitten against the warm palm of its owner.

"Thank you," says the girl, her eyes wide pools of deep blue. I notice with a strange curl of satisfaction that she's not shivering as hard now.

"Why don't you have a jacket?" I demand again, knowing I sound surly but refusing to care. Everyone else in my life has written me off as a miserable bastard and they ignore me as such—this girl might as well learn too.

At that, her mouth forms into a defensive little moue.

"It's *June*," she says. "I shouldn't need a jacket in *June*."

I stare at her like she's insane, which maybe she is.

"And the bare feet?"

"My feet got wet," she says, as if this is an entirely adequate explanation. "I didn't like it."

"You realize they've gotten even wetter without shoes."

"It's better this way," she insists, waving her shoes at me. Once I see them, I have to agree. I don't see how anyone could walk in those across the width of the shoe shop, much less along slippery, uneven pavement.

"I hope whoever you're meeting sends you home in a taxi," I mutter.

"Oh, I'm not meeting anyone," she says.

"What?"

She reaches up to brush a wet strand of hair off her cheek, but I beat her to it. I don't know why, but it's instinctive, like breathing, like blinking. Touching her.

My fingertips linger on her cheek after I brush the hair aside, and she stares up at me with something too close to trust. I drop my hand.

"I only have one night in London," she says, all that trust and big-eyed nuzzling replaced by something matter-of-fact and utterly practical. "And I spent days researching where to go for a drink tonight. It had to be within walking distance of my hotel, it had to have several five-star reviews on multiple restaurant rating sites, and it had to be established enough to have regulars but new enough to be trendy. The Goose and Gander met all of those requirements."

Well, that's where research will get you. An obnoxious

hipster cave of Edison bulbs and reclaimed wood.

"And why that specific criteria?" I ask, but I'm already peering back out into the rain, wondering if it's let up enough that I can send this crazy, shivering girl on her way. Get back to my night. My night in a dry bed with my book, alone.

Somehow it doesn't sound as appetizing as it did just a few minutes ago.

"Oh," she chirps, like she's pleased I asked. "I wanted to find a man to sleep with."

It takes a moment for her words to unfold in my brain, and I'm still staring at the rain when her meaning becomes clear. An unpleasant bolt of *something* hits me with a muffled thud.

My head swivels slowly back so I can look at her. "Excuse me?"

Her face is animated now, all red lips and high brows and dark lashes in the shadowed, rainy night. "Well, I have a plan, and I think it's a very good plan, but unfortunately my circumstances are narrowed to this one night in particular—"

"A *plan*."

She nods, that pleased look again, like I'm her star pupil.

Fuck that. *I'm* the professor here, and I have the sudden urge to tell her so. To press her against the wall and put my lips to her ear and murmur all the ways she'll respect my authority and experience.

My cock responds to the image, straining full and heavy at the thought of touching her. Teaching her. Punishing her.

"You see," she says, totally oblivious to the deviant lust pounding through me, "I really need a man with a willing penis—or I suppose I should say a willing man with a penis, but when I say it like that, it sounds very dismissive of non— You're scowling again."

She's right. "So what you're saying is that you have a plan to go to a place you've never been, in a city you've never visited, to find a man you've never met to fuck you?" My voice is frigid, bordering on cruel, and I see her blanch.

"That's very judgmental," she scolds, but I'm not to be scolded. Not right now, because I do the scolding, I make the rules, and the sooner she learns that—

Wait, no, what am I thinking? She's not going to learn anything from me. I'm not going to teach her anything. I'm not even going to spend another ten minutes with this deranged, bedraggled girl.

Even if she has the kind of long, thick hair that begs to be wrapped around a fist. Even if she has a rain-chilled body just crying to be loved warm again.

Even if she has the kind of plush red lips designed to drive men mad.

But I've been down this road before, and I know what lies at the other end of it. Bitter memories and a life left in pieces.

Never again.

"I'm judgmental because it's an idiotic idea," I reply in a sharp voice. "Do you have any idea how unsafe that is? How foolish?"

Even in the dark, I see how heat glints in her eyes, and she sticks a finger in my chest as if she's about to deliver me a scathing lecture. As she does, her arm leaves the warm confines of my jacket and reveals a delicate wrist circled with a thin band of leather.

A watch.

I don't know why that's the thing that does it, but something shears off inside my mind, sending my control bumping and careening off the tracks.

"Where's your hotel?" I ask before she can start in on whatever she was about to say.

Her brows pull together and her mouth closes. Opens again. "Why?" she asks suspiciously.

"Because I'm taking you back there."

"Why?" she asks, genuinely confused now.

"Because there's no way in hell I'm letting you prance off to a bar to find some stranger to fuck you," I say. And I give her a brief once-over, my eyes tracing where the fabric of her dress clings to her breasts and her soft belly and her achingly shaped hips. There are no secrets through that wet fabric, and those shockingly abundant curves are on clear display for anyone with eyes. For the undoubtedly many willing penises back at the pub.

The thought makes my chest tighten with something uncivilized and jealous.

"Especially not looking like *that*," I add.

Her cheeks flush dark enough that it's visible even in the night shadows, and I realize too late she thinks I'm mocking her, not warning her.

Fine. So be it. If that's what it takes to save her from the greedy arseholes at the Goose and Gander, then I'll pay the price. "What hotel?" I repeat.

She worries her bottom lip between her teeth, and that simple act has my erection throbbing against the damp fabric of my trousers, begging to be let free, begging out to play. And oh, how it could play along the soft lines of her mouth and over the wet pink of her tongue. How rude and rough it would look against the overflowing handfuls of her tits...

"The Douglass," she says finally.

"I'm staying at the Douglass too," I say before I can stop myself, and then horror curls through my chest.

She's too close.

Too real.

Too...*possible.*

*Would it be so bad?* a tiny voice whispers in my mind. *Just one night with a girl you'll never see again?*

Yes, goddammit. Yes, it would.

Meanwhile, the girl seems to be having some sort of insight. Some sort of wild epiphany. "You," she says slowly.

"What?"

"You!" Her entire face lights up. "You could be the one!"


**This story continues in**
**Misadventures with a Professor!**

# ACKNOWLEDGMENTS

I want to thank my amazing family. Michael, Mikey, Alyssa, and Gaston. Everything I do, I do it for y'all. I love you all so damn much, and nothing will ever change that. To the rest of my family, I love you.

Then my tribe, Bobbie Jo, Kristen, and Nortis. I am who I am because of you three. Thank you.

To my life manager, I love you, Holletta. Thank you for all you do.

My betas are my lifelines. They make all my books a billion times better. Laurie, Heather, Jessica, Althea, Franci, Susie, and Nicole. You are the best, I love y'all.

To my editing team: Scott and Jeanne. Thank you so much for dealing with all this crazy!

To the whole Misadventures team, thank you. Thank you so much for being the best team a girl could get.

# MORE MISADVENTURES

**VISIT MISADVENTURES.COM
FOR MORE INFORMATION!**

# MORE MISADVENTURES

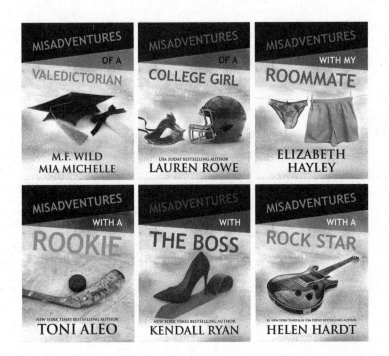